In the Cards
Love

Also by
Mariah Fredericks

Crunch Time

Head Games

The True Meaning of Cleavage

In the Cards
Love

Mariah Fredericks

aladdin **mix**

ALADDIN MIX
NEW YORK   LONDON   TORONTO   SYDNEY

This book is a work of fiction. Any references to historical events, real people, or real locales are used fictitiously. Other names, characters, places, and incidents are the product of the author's imagination, and any resemblance to actual events or locales or persons, living or dead, is entirely coincidental.

ALADDIN MIX

Simon & Schuster Children's Publishing Division

1230 Avenue of the Americas, New York, NY 10020

Text copyright © 2007 by Mariah Fredericks

Illustrations copyright © 2007 by Liselotte Watkins

All rights reserved, including the right of reproduction in whole or in part in any form.

ALADDIN PAPERBACKS and related logo are registered trademarks of Simon & Schuster, Inc.

ALADDIN MIX is a trademark of Simon & Schuster, Inc.

Designed by Ann Zeak

The text of this book was set in ITC Legacy.

Manufactured in the United States of America

First Aladdin MIX edition April 2007

2 4 6 8 10 9 7 5 3 1

The Library of Congress has cataloged the hardcover edition as follows:

Fredericks, Mariah.

Anna's story / Mariah Fredericks.

p. cm. (In the cards; #1)

"A Richard Jackson book."

Summary: Thirteen-year-old Anna hopes that her newly inherited tarot cards will predict an exciting future, including becoming the girlfriend of eighth-grade hottie Declan Kelso.

ISBN-13: 978-0-689-87654-7 (hc)

ISBN-10: 0-689-87654-8 (hc)

[1. Tarot—Fiction. 2. Fortune telling—Fiction. 3. Schools—Fiction.

4. Friendship—Fiction.] I. Title. II. Series: Fredericks, Mariah. In the cards; #1.

PZ7.F872295An 2007

[Fic]—dc22 2005031956

ISBN-13: 978-0-689-87655-4 (pbk)

ISBN-10: 0-689-87655-6 (pbk)

For Katherine Callander,
who showed me the heart of this book

PAGE of WANDS

THE HIGH PRIESTESS

THE TOWER

THE LOVERS.

PAGE of SWORDS

QUEEN of WANDS

In the Cards
Love

Sometimes I think it's all Eve's fault.

Then I think that's stupid. Just because Eve is crazy doesn't mean everything is her fault. But she was the one who said we should do it. The one who said it was lame to be scared and that we had to try it or we'd never know.

But I listened to her. So, really, it's my fault.

Other times I think Sydney's to blame. If she'd just been stronger, said, Guys, this is wrong, *maybe I wouldn't have listened to Eve.*

Only Sydney did say it was wrong, and I listened to Eve anyway. So we're back to me. It's my fault.

I hate it when things are my fault.

I try really, really hard not to let that happen. And when it does happen, I try to figure out what I did wrong, what I could have done differently. Where did I make my mistake?

Except it's not that simple. A mistake doesn't always feel like a mistake when you're making it.

For example, you can say that none of this would have happened if I hadn't taken care of Mrs. Rosemont's cats. But I couldn't say no to her. She was an old lady, she didn't have anyone else.

Eve would say I never should have even talked to Mrs. Rosemont, that she was boring and a pain. Even Syd, who's an animal freak, didn't like visiting the cats because she thought Mrs. Rosemont was strange. But you can't say to someone, Get away, you're boring! You're strange!

Well, not if you're a wimp like me.

But it is true that if I had never talked to Mrs. Rosemont in the elevator, she wouldn't have asked me to feed her cats.

And if she had never asked me to feed her cats, we wouldn't have had that talk about the future.

And if we hadn't had that talk about the future, she might not have left me these cards when she died.

Because that's where the whole thing started. The cards.

I still have them. They're in the box they came in, the leather one with the strange carvings on the top. When all the craziness was over, I put them way in the back of my closet, along with the book that explains what each of the cards means, how to read them, understand them. . . .

All I can say is, I wish we'd understood them a whole lot better.

ONE

Anna's To-Do List • Tuesday, September 22
1. Attend Act Now rally.
2. Try to sing off book in chorus. (Say something
   nice to Bridget?)
3. Ask Mr. Fegelson for an extension on biology
   project.
4. Water Mr. Kaiser's plants.
5. Walk the Dunphys' dog.
6. Get Mom to adopt Mrs. Rosemont's cats.

Does everyone think about bizarre things
when they're brushing their teeth, or is it just me?
The day after Mrs. Rosemont dies, I'm squooshing

toothpaste in my mouth when I think, *What is dead, anyway?*

Yesterday Mrs. Rosemont was here—and now she's not. But what does that mean, except I won't ever see her again?

Is she just nothing? Or is she a spirit, floating around somewhere?

Part of me thinks she's a spirit. Because I can't believe she's gone. She doesn't *feel* gone. My mom told me last night that Mrs. Rosemont died in the hospital, but I don't feel the least bit sad. It's only when I think about her cats—Beesley, Tatiana, and Mouli, lost and missing their human—that I get upset.

Which is terrible. When someone dies, you should be sad about them.

I spit, then wonder, *So, if I died tomorrow, would anybody care?*

My mom and dad would definitely freak. Russell would demand he get my room. Eve would be psyched, because it'd be all macabre and she could wear black and flip out. But then she'd get tired of it and move on to something else. Syd would be sad, though. Genuinely sad. And they'd probably do something at school, have an assembly, tell people it was okay to cry if they wanted to.

But I'm not sure how many people would cry. More likely, they'd be like, *Anna? Anna who? Oh, her. Yeah, she was . . . okay.*

My little brother Russell is waiting for me at the door. He has two pencils stuck up his nostrils. Today, apparently, he is a walrus.

Russell is seven years old, but he's been strange since the day he was born. This doesn't seem to bother most people, for example, my parents, who you'd think would be a little worried that their only son lives on a diet of tuna fish and boogers. Just the fact that he's usually pretending to be some kind of animal should raise a red flag, right? I once looked up the traits of a psychotic personality. Russell had almost every single one. I told my mother, but she said, "He's just trying to be funny, Anna. Let him have his thing." Which made me wonder, *Do I have a thing? And if so, what is it?*

On the way to school I keep thinking about Mrs. Rosemont. This is the first day she isn't here, the first day she's missing. Everything that happens from now on she won't know about. And yet we're all just going along without her.

Once she gave me a piece of butterscotch candy, and I didn't eat it because it was old and kind of sticky. But she acted like it was this big deal, like she wouldn't give this candy to anyone but me. Now I wish I'd eaten it. Even though I hate butterscotch.

As we wait for the light, Russell sways and snorts and claps his hands like they're flippers. I tell him, "Walruses smell. Walruses get fat and roll over on baby walruses and crush them." He immediately starts shrieking like a baby walrus being squished.

I will have to talk to my mother. Russell is way too casual about death.

When we get to school, Eve is waiting for me on the steps. Today she's wearing her CUTE MAKES ME GAG T-shirt. It has a picture of a kitten and a red banned circle on it. Now, if Eve died, everybody at school would remember her. I don't know if they'd cry a lot, but they'd all have an Eve story. *Remember the time she farted at the mime show? Remember when she made Ms. DeLisi cry in English class? Or the summer she chopped off all her hair?* Sometimes I worry that I'm too tame to be Eve's friend.

As we go into school, I say, "Did you hear about Mrs. Rosemont?"

"Why would I hear about Mrs. Rosemont?"

"Because she died."

Eve shrugs. "Well, she *was* like a hundred and nine."

"God, Eve . . ."

6

"Uh, hello, old woman I met twice now dead, I'm supposed to be all boohoo?" Eve sees my face, says, "Okay, okay. Sorry. God, you like . . . care about everything."

Annoyed, I say, "I don't care about everything, but she's dead, you know? Have a little respect."

Eve puts her head on my shoulder, which is her real way of saying she's sorry. "It's Act Now. It's making me borderline postal."

"I get that," I say as we head up the stairs to assembly. Because I do. Eberly, our school, is heavily into "doing things." Penny drives, donating food, cleaning up the park. Our principal, Ms. Kenworthy, has a sign on her door: A GOOD CITIZEN IS AN ACTIVE CITIZEN. So every fall they kick off the year with a big Act Now rally to tell everyone what events are planned and how they can get involved.

Which sounds great, but sometimes I wonder if Ms. Kenworthy really knows what goes on at this school. She might tell us we're all the same and not to look down on anyone, but the fact is, there are a lot of kids at Eberly who *live* to look down on people. They wouldn't have it any other way. It's absolutely understood: There's a top ruling clique, made up of the über-cool. You have to *at least* be rich and *at least* be hot—so forget it for me and Eve right there (although

I think Eve is very pretty, even if she isn't skinny-skinny and has her hair all cut up Goth style). These kids make fun of people for not wearing designer clothes, so it's a little hard to imagine them caring about the homeless.

Then, on the other end, there're the freaks, the lowest of the low. It's not as obvious how you get to be a freak. It's not about being ugly or strange or not having money—although those things help. What really does it is if you're targeted by the über-cool; if they decide to make you their little joke, you've had it. And that could happen to anybody; people try very hard at Eberly to stay out of the Freak Zone, which usually means joining in on the torture of existing freaks.

This is why I'm not sure if Ms. Kenworthy has the least clue. She should. All she has to do is look out and see how everyone's sitting. Über-cools like Chris Abernathy and his Cro-Magnonic bud Kyle are, of course, near the P&Ps (what Eve calls the "pretty and perfects") like Elissa Maxwell and Alexa Roth. Whereas Crazy Nelson Kobliner is sitting all the way off to the side, as is Planet Janet Epstein. (Janet's a little . . . heavy.) If Ms. Kenworthy did take the time to look, she'd see Chris pitching a balled-up Chinese menu at Janet right now. She'd see Elissa giggling and pointing at Sara Reynolds's hand-me-down sweater.

She'd also see Declan Kelso, as well as every girl in school staring at Declan Kelso. Declan is, without question, the hottest guy at Eberly. And not just in the eighth grade, either. I bet there are sophomores who would date Declan.

And what's really funny is that up until this year, Declan was a major freak. Not even a freak—a *geek*. You know Ark-Ark on *Ovidian Planet*? The dorky alien who's always screwing up? That's what Declan looked like. People actually *called* him "Ark-Ark." They knocked his books out of his arms, drew on his clothes with pen, and repeated whatever he said in a retarded voice until he almost cried. Some people found it quite hilarious.

But this year, when he came back to school, nobody recognized him. He was taller, wider—"babe shaped," as Lara Tierney put it. The glasses were gone, so everyone could see he had big blue eyes with the longest lashes. The brown hair was a little longer, so it didn't stick out anymore. The old Declan was always making weird jokes nobody laughed at. This Declan doesn't say much, just goes around with his head down and his hands jammed in the pockets of his army jacket.

Declan is the first major crossover from freak to über-cool, and every girl in school is crazy about him.

The P&Ps think he's a babe, but geek girls think they have a chance because he used to be one of us. Naturally, everyone wants to see which girl he'll ask out, what group she'll belong to. It's a big topic of discussion on Zoe's World, a Web site run by official school gossip Zoe Friedlander. She even has a list of top candidates of future G.O.D.s (Girlfriends of Declan).

Needless to say, my name is not on the list. I'd like to say I don't care. That I find all this fuss over Declan Kelso pathetic and that, really, he's not *that* cute. . . .

But I'd be lying. I think he's amazing.

Frankly, I thought Declan was cute when he was Ark-Ark. Only I wasn't going to ask Ark-Ark out, right? Serves me right, because he's way beyond me now.

Ms. Kenworthy stands up and taps the microphone. "People, could we all calm down now and give our full attention to the matter at hand?"

Despite the fact that I think she's clueless about certain things, I sort of admire Ms. Kenworthy. All the things she wants us to think about are good things, and she is very . . . forceful. She's the kind of person you can imagine as a statue one day.

Now she says, "We have many exciting events planned for this semester. This year for Halloween, instead of the traditional dance, we will ask students to take to the streets in costume to ask for donations to Habitat for Humanity."

Eve frowns. "Whoa, no Halloween dance? That sucks."

Over the murmur of disappointment, Ms. Kenworthy says, "For those of you saddened by the loss of the Halloween dance, you will be happy to know that at the Thanksgiving Harvest Festival, in addition to our canned goods drive, we will have the first annual Eberly Turkey Trot and then our usual holiday party just before the start of winter break."

Oh. No. *The Turkey Trot?* Is she kidding? If it were anybody but Ms. Kenworthy, people would boo.

Raising her voice, Ms. Kenworthy says, "Finally, as we start this school year, I'd like each of us to think about how we could be kinder to one another. Humanity can be expressed in many ways. Even by reaching out to someone we don't know and asking them to lunch."

Hmm. Maybe Ms. Kenworthy isn't so out of it after all. Without thinking, I look over at Nelson Kobliner. Since Declan went "GreekGod"—Zoe's name for him—Nelson is now officially the weirdest guy in school. He's got a strange jar-shaped head, and he's always getting into fights. Kids might ask for donations to charity, but no way is anyone asking Nelson Kobliner to lunch.

Then Ms. Kenworthy says, "Thank you," and everyone is up and headed for the door. As Eve and I struggle to make our way through the crowd, I see Declan edging along his row to join the aisle. If I time it right, he will reach the aisle just as we pass.

I know it's dumb. I know I have no shot. And yet, I slow down. Because—I don't know. It can't be coincidence that we're about to collide like this. Eve pulls on my arm, but I don't speed up. Just a few more seconds . . .

I feel someone pass behind me and look up. It's Crazy Nelson Kobliner, and instinctively, I back off. Maybe it's mean of me, but there is something scary about Nelson. He's so big, and it seems like he's always about to hit something. He carries this weird battered notebook everywhere. I can't imagine what's in it.

Then I feel bad. Two minutes after Ms. Kenworthy told us to be nicer to people, I'm already dissing Nelson. I try to smile at him, but he scowls and shoves past me. As he does, I move to make room and bump right up against Declan.

Which is totally perfect. But as I turn around, I hear, "Hey, Anna, ready to take over the altos this year?" The voice is Southern. And loud. And about three feet over my head.

It is Mr. Courtney, music teacher and chorus master.

It's useless to pretend I didn't hear Mr. Courtney; everyone hears Mr. Courtney. But I have to try—and I have to hope Declan didn't hear him. Because I do not want Declan finding out I am in chorus.

If being ugly or strange is a good way to join the Freak Zone, being in chorus is even better. It's a well-established fact that only losers, nerds, and geeks sing in chorus. But I've been in it since second grade because I like singing, even though I'm not so good.

Mr. Courtney has only been here a year. Old chorus teachers knew chorus was uncool and put up with what they got. Courtney is always trying to recruit people. Now, totally blocking the aisle so Eve, Declan, and I are trapped in front of him, he says to Eve, "You gonna sing in my chorus?"

Eve narrows her eyes. "Uh, how about I would not be caught dead?"

"Wouldn't be caught dead? Gal, you don't join my chorus, I'll catch you and kill you. Declan, when you coming to chorus?" Declan does a little half smile, shrugs. "You *want* to be in chorus, believe me. You want to meet girls, right? Well, the best girls are in my chorus. Girls like Anna Morris here. . . ."

I cannot even look Declan in the face. Someone please tell me: What did I do to deserve humiliation at the hands of Mr. Courtney? Meanwhile, Mr. Courtney's still yelling: "Still time to change your schedule, you know. I expect to see a whole bunch of you young men in my chorus next week."

Then he strides back down the aisle. For a long, awful, weird moment, Declan and I just stand there. Then I smile. Because maybe he's standing there for a reason, maybe he wanted to talk to me. . . .

Only Declan doesn't smile back. He says, "Sorry— can I get by?"

I leap aside. "Uh, sure. Sorry."

"Thanks." As he steps past me, I pray that no one saw me make a total fool of myself.

But my prayer is not answered as Eve says, "Okay, how long were we going to keep *that* little secret?"

Clutching my book bag, I mutter, "I don't . . . like him or anything."

"Oh, please. You went bovine."

"I did not," I say, even as I think, *Oh, God, did I?*

"You did," she says menacingly. "This *will* be discussed."

And from her tone, I know, I *will not* enjoy the discussion.

TWO

Zoe's World, 9/22
Who Shall Be G.O.D.?
Vote for the girl most likely to succeed
with Declan Kelso:
1. Elissa Maxwell
2. Alexa Roth
3. Chloe Deutscher
4. Jackie Gonzalez

All morning I am petrified that the entire school witnessed my humiliation. As often as I tell myself that the one good thing about being a blah nobody is that people couldn't care less what you do, I'm convinced that everybody knows I have a crush on Declan—including Declan.

I know I shouldn't worry, that I should just forget it, act like it never happened. Mrs. Rosemont said that to me once, that I worried way too much. "Anna, you're young. You shouldn't have so many worries. Life takes care of itself, you'll see." I remember thinking, *Okay, but who takes care of everything else?*

My terror that I have been exposed as Sad Girl Who Likes Declan isn't helped when I walk into biology and Alexa Roth and Marnie Stonor immediately start giggling. Alexa whispers something to Marnie; Marnie whispers back. I bite down hard, tell myself they are not whispering about me.

But I know they are. If I am Sad Girl Who Likes Declan, Alexa is Hot Girl Who Likes Declan. She's been on Zoe's list of G.O.D. candidates from the very beginning. She's very pretty, with blue eyes and dark hair that looks almost black. Plus, she's an actress. A real one; she's been in commercials—well, one cat food ad—but she's always going on auditions for movies and TV shows. Naturally, she expects to get the lead in every school play, sulks when she doesn't, and backstabs whoever does. Last year, when she didn't get to be Sandy in *The Prime of Miss Jean Brodie,* she offered to help Christa Matthews, who did get the part—and then went around telling everyone how bad Christa was.

Of all the girls Declan could date, I really, really hope he doesn't pick Alexa. She's too nasty to deserve anything good happening to her.

Trying to ignore Alexa and Marnie, I check out the pictures Mr. Fegelson has on the walls. There's a shot of a tiger with enormous yellow eyes that reminds me of Mouli, the wildest of Mrs. Rosemont's cats. She coaxed him from the street, but he never liked to be held and hissed if you came near him. I think of him as Psycho Mouli. Then there's Tatiana, a regal Persian that hangs off your arm like a luxurious wrap, and Beesley, the oldest, a creaky old calico.

I wonder where they are now, Tat, Beesley, and Mouli. If Mrs. Rosemont didn't tell someone what to do with them, they could just end up in a shelter—and we all know what that means. Last night I begged my mom to take them in. Not to keep, just until we found them homes. She said no, absolutely not. "Honey, I know you want to do something, but there isn't anything you can do. Human beings don't have as much power as you might think they do."

Which makes me nuts, because there is something she could do—she just doesn't want to. But I'm going to keep working on her.

Next to the tiger is a timeline of the earth. It shows how long it took the earth to cool, how long dinosaurs were around. At the end there's this tiny green part where human beings come into the story. It's weird, how short a time we've been here. You think how short each life is, and your head really starts spinning. Mrs. Rosemont would be the teeniest, tiniest sliver on that chart. You probably wouldn't even see her.

I think, *Mrs. Rosemont, you made sure your little guys were safe, right?*

After biology I have English with Ms. Taramini. This is the first time I've had her, and I don't know what to think of her yet. Everyone says she's a harsh grader; you either love her or hate her. Usually, I get along okay with teachers, but she never smiles when I raise my hand, never says *Good point* or anything. I have a weird feeling she doesn't like me for some reason.

We're reading *Oedipus Rex*, which is about a guy who's told by the gods that he'll do awful things in his life, and no matter how hard he tries to avoid it, he does them anyway. While Peta Talbot says it's just gross to be reading about a guy who kills his father and marries his mother, I make a list for my mother of reasons we should take the cats.

I'm a list person. Every morning I make a list of

things to do that day and cross them off as I go along. I also make lists for big things. Like, every New Year, I make resolutions. Change this, be more that. Eve says it's a sign of a sick mind. But the way I see it, with a list, I know what to do—and when everything's crossed off, I know I've done it.

Under *Why We Should Adopt the Cats*, I write,

1. *It will only be until we can find them new homes.*
2. *Will be good for Russell to have responsibilities.*
3. *They're helpless. We can help them.*

I'm trying to think of how to get around my mom's claim that she has allergies when Ms. Taramini asks, "Who here, if they could know the future, would choose to know?"

Which reminds me of the last conversation I ever had with Mrs. Rosemont. It was about the future. Just a few days ago she was telling me one of her "When I Was a Child" stories, and I must have said the wrong thing—like *That's nice* when I should've said *That's awful.*

But she laughed and said, "You're young. You don't care about the past. . . . Only now." She stepped closer. "And the future, maybe?"

All of a sudden, she was so intense. I said, "Yeah, I think about the future. Wonder what'll happen."

She peered at me. "You'd like to know what will happen?"

"Sometimes. Sometimes I think, 'Uh, maybe not.'"

She laughed again. "Smart girl. But you'll figure it out. The past and the present—they are the future. You can see the future, you're making it happen right now."

Now I think, *Well, Mrs. Rosemont, if that's true, I wish you'd said,* Go not to school on Tuesday. Avoid the boy with blue eyes! Doom and despair will follow if you fail to heed my advice!

And, Mrs. Rosemont? If you can see the future, can you tell me if maybe someday I won't be boring, blah Anna? Anna who sings in chorus? Anna who feeds cats—not that I ever minded feeding your cats. Or maybe if I am all those things, could I still be the kind of person the occasional exciting thing happens to? Not a million things. Just . . . you know . . . well, you know what I mean.

I look up at the ceiling, but there's no answer. Wherever Mrs. Rosemont is, I guess they don't let you phone home.

After school Eve and her parents have a meeting with Ms. Kenworthy to discuss her "attitude" this year. Eve calls it the "Don't Burn Down the Building speech." Russell has a judo class, so I'm on my own. Eve's going to call me when she gets home.

I'm nervous of what Eve's going to say about the Declan thing. Our deal at school is that we don't get stupid about the stuff everyone else does. We don't care what Elissa is wearing, we don't tell Alexa if we saw her commercial, and we don't go crazy for boys everyone is crazy for. Eve thinks Declan-mania is for losers. So I've kind of broken the rules by liking him.

I wonder if I could tell Syd about our fight. I don't want her to pick sides or anything. But if Eve's in a rude mood, it might help to have Syd back me up. She goes to a different school and sometimes sees our fights more clearly than I do. It's funny how different Eve and Syd are. If I weren't friends with both of them, I'm not sure they'd be friends at all. Syd is very shy, but if you're her friend or a stray animal, she is totally there for you. Sometimes she's braver about standing up to Eve than I am.

When I get home, I just drop my bag on the floor and leave it—even though my mom hates that. Normally, I like having the house to myself, but today it feels lonely. Like the apartment's sitting there, silent and deserted, saying, *So, what are you going to do, Anna?*

If Eve were here and we weren't fighting, we'd be

watching VH1 and planning her meteoric rise to fame and my fabulous life as her manager/sidekick.

If Syd were here, we could ride bikes or something. But Syd has piano.

If Russell were here, I'd be trying to keep him from making obscene phone calls—something my mother does not know he does because, so far, I have gotten him off the phone before they're able to trace the call.

This is one of the times I wish my parents weren't divorced and that my dad still lived with us instead of across town. He's a restaurant chef, so when I was little, he'd be home a lot because he mostly worked nights. When I came home from school, we'd try out all these weird recipes. Now we only do that every other weekend.

I look over at my computer. This summer I promised myself I would not look at Zoe's World. All Zoe's World does is make you believe nasty things about other people and feel rotten that you're not interesting enough to be gossiped about.

But I feel like I should check to make sure she didn't write anything about me being a goof with Declan. I'm sure she didn't; I'm hardly worth her notice. But Zoe does write about everything Declan does, so . . .

Just a quick peek.

Except for the Declan Watch List, Zoe doesn't do

names, just descriptive nicknames like "WeedBoy" for Peter Henninger or "Diva" for Alexa Roth. That way, the people she's talking about can never get mad at her because she just says, "Oh, that wasn't you." I'm scared to think what she'd call me.

Oh, God, here it is.

Anybody spot ChorusGrl get burned by GreekGod in assembly? Two mistakes, ChorusGrl: actually being *in* chorus—hello, how many times do we need to hear "The Water Is Wide"?—and hanging with GoofyGothGrl.

Who knows, though? Make a few changes, and things might be very different. . . .

ChorusGrl? CHORUSGRL? Gee, thanks, Zoe. Why not flat out call me "GeekGrl" or "FreakGrl," since that's what you meant? And telling me to dump my best friend? Very nice. Very über-cool.

And another thing. Why is she telling me to make some changes and things could be different? Yeah, ChorusGrl: Change every single thing about yourself, and maybe, *maybe*, we'll deign to find you acceptable—*not*.

I'm wondering if it's worth posting something

really nasty back when the doorbell rings. My first thought is it's the Stranger. As in, the one you're not supposed to open the door to. Immediately, I shut down Zoe's World. If it is a serial killer, I don't want people knowing the last thing I did on this earth is check out a cheesy gossip page.

I walk down the hall, go up to the door, and peer through the hole.

But it's not the Stranger. It's Ruben, our doorman.

I open the door, say, "Hey, Ruben. What's up?"

Ruben smiles. "I have a package for you."

"For me?" I never get packages. "What is it?"

He holds up a little box. Even from here, I can see it's old. The leather's all worn, and it has weird images on it. It looks like it would smell funny, like it's from another country.

He says, "You know Mrs. Rosemont passed, right?" I nod. "She left a note, saying she wanted you to have this."

I'm about to take it when I hear something meow and notice there's another box at Ruben's feet. It's moving. Like something is inside it, and it's seriously ticked off. I lean down, peer in. I see a fat orange face, hear a hiss.

"Oh," says Ruben. "And this."

I stare at him. "She gave me Psycho Mouli?"

Ruben laughs. "Sure did."

I look around. "What about the other cats?"

"I don't know. They went to other places. She left phone numbers, I made the calls. You're the only one in the building."

Oh, man. Why couldn't Mrs. Rosemont give me Tat? Or even Beesley? Why Psycho Mouli?

How many ways can my mother murder me at once?

Ruben says, "If you don't want him, I have to take him to the shelter." Mouli hisses. Guess he knows what "shelter" means.

"No, don't. I'll . . ."

I put out my hands. In one, Ruben puts the carrier. In the other, the little brown box.

I take Mouli back to my room. Kneeling on the floor, I tell him, "Okay, the deal is this. Complete and absolute silence until I can figure out how to tell my mom about you. You put one paw outside my bedroom before I say so, and you're meat. Because, basically, I'm meat."

Behind the grille, Mouli has gone quiet. Saying, "Remember. We have a deal," I pull the latch open.

But he just stays inside the carrier. For a moment I feel really bad for him. His friends are gone suddenly; he's in this whole new house. I must seem like his worst nightmare.

Then I notice there's a card on top of the carrier. Taking it off, I open it. It reads:

For Anna. Who is mindful.

Then I look at the other thing Mrs. Rosemont left me.

It's a very peculiar box. It's definitely from somewhere else, but I can't guess where. There are flowers and birds carved on to the top. It looks like once they were painted red, yellow, and green, but most of the color is faded now.

Very carefully, I shake it. A soft sliding sound, then a knock as whatever it is hits the side.

Could be a ring. Except it doesn't sound like a ring.

I set it down on the rug, sit in front of it with my legs crossed.

I ask, *What are you?*

The box doesn't answer.

I do not want to be alone when I open this box. Whom to call? Eve or Syd? Some things are Eve things and some are Syd things. Horror movies and sabotaging the makeup counter at Macy's are Eve things. Bike riding and anytime I want to talk when I'm not sure I make sense are Syd things.

Mrs. Rosemont's gift is definitely a Both thing.

I call Sydney, say, "Are you done with piano?"

"Yeah, why?"

"You have to come over right now."

"Why? What happened?"

I look at Mouli. "I can't explain on the phone. You just have to see it."

"Should I call the police?"

"No, no. Just come over."

Then I call Eve, keeping my fingers crossed that she's home. When she picks up, I say, "Come over. Right now. Something really strange just happened."

"Really?" Even over the phone, I can hear Eve is excited. "Be right over."

Eve lives five blocks away. Syd lives in the building, so she arrives first. When I open the door, she says breathlessly, "Are you okay?"

"Yeah, no, I'm fine. Really. Come in." She does, looking around like a burglar is going to leap out at her. I shouldn't have sounded so scared on the phone.

I say, "It's in my room."

Syd doesn't even notice the box. Instead, she goes straight to the carrier, crying, "Oh, my God, you got a cat." I hear Mouli hiss, then a thud as he recoils to the back of the cage. Syd turns to me. "Poor thing is *so* upset. How'd you get him?"

"Remember Mrs. Rosemont?"

"Creepy Mrs. Rosemont on the twelfth floor?"

"Who just died?" Syd makes a "Sorry" face; she didn't know. "She left him to me."

"Awesome," says Syd happily. If the world had half as many humans and twice as many animals, Syd would be a happy girl. "Is this what you wanted me to see?"

"Not exactly. . . ." Then the bell rings, and I have to go let Eve in.

THREE
SHE WHO WOULD THE FUTURE KNOW . . .

"So, she left you a psycho cat and an ugly box."

This is Eve's reaction to my story of Mrs. Rosemont's gifts.

Syd has been trying to lure Mouli out of his carrier with water and little bits of tuna. Now she says, "It's not ugly. What's in it?"

"I have no idea. That's why I wanted you guys here."

We all look at it.

I say, "Mrs. Rosemont wouldn't leave me anything dangerous, right?"

Eve says solemnly, "You never know. Maybe it contains the plague that will destroy all mankind."

Syd shoots her a look. "It's probably jewelry. Or even empty. Just a nice box to keep things in."

"No, there's something inside," I tell her. "You can hear it."

We sit there for a few more minutes, then Eve says, "Well, this is lame. Come on, open it."

But I can't. So, of course, Eve reaches for the box. But Syd says, "I think Anna has to. She's the one Mrs. Rosemont left it to."

"Fine." Eve puts the box in my lap.

For a moment I hesitate. Then I remember Mrs. Rosemont thrusting the piece of butterscotch candy into my hand, and I feel ashamed I could think she would leave me something dangerous. Carefully putting two thumbs on either side of the lid, I coax the box open. When it's loose, I take the top off, lay it on the floor.

There's a little scroll inside the box. It's old and yellow. I'm worried if I open it, it'll turn to dust. Very carefully, I tug it straight. It says,

> *She who would the future know*
> *Deep into the past must go.*
> *To see where her future lies,*
> *Behold the present with clear eyes.*

It's in calligraphy. The letters are strong and clear. I think of Mrs. Rosemont's hands, how they were all bunched up and gnarled like claws. I can't imagine her writing this. But if she didn't, who did? The way it's written, it could be from fifty years ago. Or hundreds.

Under the scroll, there's a green velvet bag. I take it out. It's heavy with something that feels like a little book inside. I hold it in the palm of my hand, run my fingers along the side. The book shifts, slides, becomes . . . cards.

I tug open the drawstring, pull the cards out. They look nothing like ordinary playing cards. For one thing, they're bigger. And instead of hearts and spades, some have these weird circles, and others have swords and others these long pole things and others something like a bowl.

A lot of them have these very intricate drawings of people. I turn a few of them over. All of a sudden, a devil with nasty horns is leering up at me. I put the deck down.

Eve picks it up. Thumbing through the deck, she says, "They're tarot cards."

Syd looks but keeps her distance. "What do they do?"

"They tell the future." Eve wiggles her eyebrows. Pulling the Devil card out, she holds it up. I can't help it, it's so ugly, I pull back.

"Ooh," says Eve, pulling out another card, a knight on horseback. His face is a skull. "Death."

Uneasy, I say, "Come on, don't make fun of them."

"I'm not making fun of them. These are serious, man. They used to be banned. People said it was witchcraft." She puts them back in the bag, hands them to me. "Why do you think Rosemont wanted *you* to have them?"

Syd says, "Obviously, because Anna was nice to her and she wanted to say thank you."

"No," I say, fingering the velvet. "That's not why."

I can feel Syd and Eve looking at me, but since I don't really know what I mean, I can't explain it to them. All I know is that this is more than a thank-you.

"So," says Eve. "Let's do a reading."

"How? We don't have the first clue."

Eve picks up the box. At the bottom, although I didn't see it before, there's a small book. "This probably tells you how."

"Careful," I say, taking it from her. I see it has diagrams that show you how to lay out the cards. Then all these little definitions. Two of Wands—those must be the poles. Three of Pentacles . . .

"Aren't pentacles what you use to call up the devil?" I say.

"That's penta*grams*," says Eve. "Come on, let's do it."

"No, don't," says Syd suddenly. "I don't think you should play around with stuff like this."

I say, "They're just cards, Syd. It's like a Ouija board." Which we did once. We tried to contact Syd's grandfather. Eve swears she didn't move the planchette, that it was spirits or whatever, but I know for a fact, her hands were moving it. Besides, if it was Syd's grandfather, all he said was "Urgl." Which wasn't very illuminating.

Then I notice Mouli has stuck his head out of the carrier. But not to get a drink of water. He's watching me. I feel like he's speaking to me. *What are you waiting for?*

I look again at the scroll.

> *To see where her future lies,*
> *Behold the present with clear eyes.*

All of a sudden, Mouli leaps onto my desk. Both Syd and Eve jump. He sits there, tail twitching, looking straight at me.

"We have to do it," I say. "It would be wrong not to."

"Excellent!" Eve snatches up the book. "Okay, first thing is to pick a question."

"A question."

"Yeah, you have to tell them what you want to know. So, what do you want to know?"

Both Syd and Eve look at me. I'm starting to wish one of them were going first. I mean, this is getting a little personal.

I think. "Um . . . am I going to do well on next week's math test?"

"Bo-ring," says Eve.

"Let her pick, it's her question," says Syd.

"No, okay, wait." I think again. "Will I go to Mexico with my dad this summer?"

Eve breathes deeply like she's making some massive effort to control herself. "No. Forget school, forget parents and vacation and all that kind of junk. This is for real. Think about life. Fame. Love . . ." She claps her hands, points to me. "That's *it*. That is totally it."

Syd and I look at each other like, *Okay, Eve has finally lost her mind.*

I ask, "What's it?"

"Declan." She explains to Syd, "This guy Anna's madly in love with."

I stare at her.

Eve says, "Come on, you know you want to know."

I almost laugh. But then I don't. Because I do want to know. I want to know if I have any hope, in spite of the Elissas and Alexas and every other girl in our class.

I look up at Eve. Normally, she would never approve of asking about something as goopy as a boy. I wonder why she's decided it's okay.

Then I look down at the cards. Am I really going to do this? It can't hurt. The cards are silly. Me liking Declan or thinking he would ever like me is totally silly. So it all sort of goes together.

"Okay," I say. "Let's ask about Declan."

Eve opens the book to the diagram that shows how to lay out the cards. Mouli is still on the desk. He seems to be sleeping. Like, *Humans and their problems, what could be more yawn-inducing?*

Eve hands me the deck. "The book says to shuffle them thoroughly while you meditate upon your question."

"Okay . . ." I break the deck into two halves.

Eve says, "Wait, there has to be a ritual."

Syd stares at her. "Like what, Mistress of the Dark?"

"Like . . . an incantation. Something to let the universe know we're starting." Eve closes her eyes. "Oh, Powers of the Beyond, grant us the answers we seek. . . ."

Part of me wants to laugh. And part of me wants Eve to shut up because she's getting way too freaky.

Sydney swallows. "Guys, I'm creeped out."

Actually, I am too. It's too weird that this deck is from someone who died yesterday.

Mrs. Rosemont gave you the deck because she wanted you to use it.

But what if it's evil? What if it's all about death and devils and weirdness?

Eve finishes her chant, opens her eyes. "Okay. Go."

I start shuffling. I am not a good shuffler. I wonder what it means if the cards go kasplat all over the room: *Sorry, you don't get your wish. And by the way, you're cursed for life.*

Meditate upon your question. *Okay, will I . . . ?*

I think of Declan in the library, pushing his glasses up. Declan smiling. Graffiti in the bathroom: DECLAN KELSO IS THE HOTTEST GUY ON EARTH!

Will I . . . ?

To be fair, I think about all the reasons Declan would never be into me. I think about all the girls who are so much hotter than me. How I am a nerd girl and should restrict my interest to nerd boys only. . . .

Will I . . . ?

I think of assembly today, everything around my meeting with Declan: Mr. Courtney, creepy Nelson Kobliner . . .

Will I . . . ?

"You have to say your question out loud," says Eve. "So we can all hear it."

I do a last shuffle, feel the cards flutter into place. Say out loud, "Will I be with Declan Kelso?"

Take the first card, lay it down. . . .

Syd reads over my shoulder, then checks the book. "The High Priestess. Is that you?"

"I don't know." I lay the next card down sideways over it like the book shows. "The Eight of Wands. Is this making sense to anybody yet?"

"Do the whole thing," says Eve, staring at the two cards. "Then we'll figure out what it means."

I do, quickly laying down seven more cards. I hesitate, then lay down the last one, the one that's supposed to be your ultimate destiny card. When she sees it, Eve says, "Oh, my God."

It's the Lovers.

Even Syd is staring now. "That's wild."

It is wild. It's totally wild. But one of us has to get a grip here. Trying to sound practical, I say, "Okay, let's just . . . start at the beginning. Card number one . . ."

"That's your present position," says Eve, reading from the book. "Like what you're doing now."

I look at the card. To judge by the picture on it, I'm wearing a bizarre hat and sitting between two pillars. "What does the High Priestess mean?" I ask Eve.

"Wisdom, knowledge . . ."

"That's definitely you," says Syd. "Ms. Intellectual." I smile at her.

". . . secrecy," Eve continues. "That's not you—you can never keep a secret."

"How do you know?" I say with a small smile.

Eve rolls her eyes, reads, "'The querent, if female.'"

Syd laughs. "The querent?"

"Yeah, like questioner," I say. "Or query."

"Okay, wise querent. So this is you. You're like this smart, wise chick who keeps secrets. Check. And this card"—Eve points to the one I laid sideways over the High Priestess—"is your immediate influence. Like either what's pushing you ahead or blocking your path." Eve turns the pages. "Only . . ."

"What?"

"Well, the cards mean one thing if they're right side up and another if they're upside down. But since this card is sideways, I can't tell which way it's going."

Syd says, "So read both definitions, and we'll pick whichever one seems right."

Eve rolls her eyes. "Hello, you can't pick one. This is fate. Okay, right side up, the Eight of Wands means great hope. Also"—Eve wiggles her eyebrows—"the arrows of love."

Syd says, "Oh, my God, weird."

I don't want to feel how weird it is, so I say, "What about if it's upside down?"

Eve lowers her voice. "Arrows of jealousy. Dispute. Quarrels."

"So which one's right?" Syd wants to know.

"Oh, man . . . ," I murmur. I'm definitely hopeful that arrows of love will come winging my way and also zap Declan at the same time. On the other hand, I can't just decide the happy one is true because I want it to be.

But I don't think I'm a wildly jealous person. Not really. I never fight with anyone. Except with Eve, who fights with everyone. And even then, I'm always the one who makes up because I hate it when people are mad at each other.

Eve says, "Really, the first one makes more sense, since you're so *madly* in love with Declan already. You are awaiting romance yet to come," she says solemnly, as if she's some sort of Madame Zara, Queen of the Fortune-Tellers.

Syd giggles. "Deep."

"What's this one?" I point to the Tower card under the first two because it looks scary. It's a picture of a tower being zapped by lightning.

Eve consults the book. "That's your past. Your distant past."

"Excellent. What does it mean?"

"Chaos, things falling apart. Everything you thought was okay suddenly turns to caca."

"Wow," says Syd. "Who knew your life was so dramatic?"

"Yeah." I smile. "I think that one could be wrong."

"Come on, something must have happened. The cards do not lie." I can tell, Eve has already decided she's the one who knows all about the cards.

"No, really. I have a pretty boring life."

"Your parents did get divorced," says Syd.

I say, "Like, everyone's parents are divorced." Although that's not true. Neither Syd's nor Eve's parents have split up. Syd's parents do fight a lot, and sometimes we wonder if they will divorce someday. Or maybe should divorce.

"I don't think it was that big a thing," I say. "I was nine. I don't even remember much about it."

This is not absolutely true. I do remember a lot about it. But it's not like I'm traumatized.

"Still," says Eve authoritatively. "In the area of love and romance, you may have to accept the fact that you're a deeply damaged human being."

"From you, that could almost be a compliment."

"It could, actually," Eve agrees. "Okay, moving on. This is your recent past." She points to the card to the left of the first two in the middle. It's the Six of Cups upside down.

I say, "Is that bad?"

"Not necessarily," says Eve mysteriously. "Upside down, this card means new opportunities—or it means plans that might fail."

I demand, "Well, which one?" Because it makes a big difference. Either my meeting with Declan today was an opportunity or something that failed. Then I think: *They are just cards, Anna! Chill out!*

"We must look to the other cards," says Eve serenely.

Syd laughs, gets up to pet Mouli. But as she approaches, he leaps off the desk and runs under my bed. She says, "I guess he's upset about Mrs. Rosemont."

"Or," says Eve, "he doesn't want you disturbing his concentration during the reading." She points to the next two cards, one on top of the center pair and one to the right of it. "These two are about your future."

I say, "Gettin' to the good part," to cover up how nervous I'm feeling.

"This one"—Eve points to the one on top—"is your immediate future, what's coming right up."

Syd peeks. "It's a guy."

Eve reads aloud: "'The Page of Wands is loyal, kind, and trustworthy. He is a *dark young man.*'"

"Oh, my God." I explain to Syd, "Declan has dark hair."

"It also says he's a scholar," Eve adds meaningfully. "And a lov-ah."

I will never, ever say they're just cards again. I can't believe it. This is getting so crazy.

"How do you know it's Declan?" Syd asks. "I mean, lots of guys have dark hair."

"It's totally Declan," says Eve. "Believe me, if you knew him, you'd see it."

"Go on," I say. "What's the next card?"

The next card is a heart with three swords through it. It looks horribly painful. Eve says, "This is like your future influence. What's going to have an effect on you in the future." She looks at the book. "Hmm . . ."

I guess: "Not great?"

"Uh, not wildly fabulous, no." She reads quickly: "'Strife, unhappiness, sorrow, opposition, disappointment.' In other words, total bummer."

For a moment we all sit there. My big romance is ruined before it even got started.

Then I think: *You don't know that. The cards could be wrong.*

But if I think they're right when they say the Page

of Wands is going to show up, then I have to admit they're right when the Three of Swords says things will get sucky.

Rats.

Syd points out, "Yeah, but you get the Lovers at the end of the whole thing. Don't lovers have to go through trial and tribulation before they're happy?"

"Totally," says Eve. "It's a rule."

"What do the rest of them say?" I point to the line of four cards that ends in the Lovers. "How do we get to the good stuff?"

Eve consults the book. "This card down at the bottom is how you see yourself. The Queen of Wands."

"Hey," says Syd, "like the Page of Wands."

Eve shoots her a look. Then says to me, "Apparently, you see yourself as kind, interested in others, devoted . . ."

Yeah, I think most of that's true.

" . . . *chaste* . . ."

I go completely red.

" . . . practical, blah, blah, blah. Moving on. This card"—she taps the next one in line—"is how other people see *you*."

Oh, boy. It's The Page of Swords, but upside down. So people see me as a boy with a sword hanging upside down. Great.

"Wait," says Syd. "How *who* sees her? It depends on the person, doesn't it? Like, I don't see Anna the same way Russell sees Anna."

"I assume it's how Declan sees her," says Eve loftily.

"So," I say, "let's get it over with."

Eve turns the page, looks startled. "Impostor . . ."

"Oh, please," says Sydney.

"What else?" I ask.

"Uh . . ." Eve is embarrassed. "Powerlessness in the face of stronger forces. Unprepared."

So Declan looks at me and another girl—Alexa, say—and thinks, *Well, Anna's sort of cute, but Alexa is a mega actress babe.* I say, "That actually makes sense."

"How?" Syd asks.

"It just does. What's the next card?"

"Your hopes and fears. More swords . . ." It's the Ten of Swords. "Okay, this is really bad, but it's your fears, not what's going to happen." I nod. "It's like ruin, desolation, misery, disappointment . . . that all makes sense, right? Let's get to your final destiny . . . the Lovahs! Love, passion, fabulousness . . ."

I laugh. "It doesn't say that. Read what it really says."

Eve does. "'Beginning of romance . . . the need for being tested.' And all that other stuff, too—I didn't make that up."

Syd sits back down. She crosses her legs, fixes her chin on her fist as she looks at the cards. "It really is pretty amazing. The way it all comes together."

"You are going to be with Declan Kelso," announces Eve.

I stare at the cards. The Tower, the heart stabbed with swords, the Page of Wands. "Do you really think that's Declan?"

"Of course," says Eve. "You asked about Declan. Who else would it be?"

"Yeah . . ." I asked about Declan, but while I was thinking, a lot of other stuff came into my head. A young man with dark hair, though, that is Declan.

I start gathering up the cards, but Syd says, "Wait, we should write it down. That way, you'll remember it if it starts coming true."

She gets her notebook out of her bag, starts sketching the cards. She writes and draws very neatly. While she copies the reading, I ask Eve, "So you're not pissed that I like Declan?"

Eve draws her finger along the designs carved on top of the box. "At first I thought it was pretty lame. But then I started thinking—everyone just assumes Declan's going to go for some P&P. How awesome would it be if he didn't? If he stayed true to his own and chose a freak instead?"

"Gee, thanks." Even though I know that from Eve, "freak" is not an insult.

"No, seriously. What if, for once, the losers won out against the über-cools? GeekGrl gets GreekGod? It'd turn the school upside down." Eve raises her fist. "Fight for the freaks! And, I figure, what better freak than you?"

Then she says casually, "But I think you have to change some stuff."

Immediately, I remember what Zoe said. I wonder if Eve knows the changes she had in mind.

"Like what stuff?"

"Like your . . ." Eve lifts her hands. "Your look. Or sort of . . . overall . . . nonlook." She scrambles up, grabs my hand. "Come here a sec."

Eve drags me over to the mirror. I cringe, hating the sight of myself.

"Here we have a ponytail"—she tugs on my hair—"and a sweater I'm guessing Mom bought?" I nod. "Jeans, sneakers, the whole nice girl look. None of it's *bad*, but it's all kind of blah." She peers at me. "Do you get what I'm saying?"

"You're saying I'm blah."

"And that's cool, that's fine—well, it's pretty boring, actually. But if you're going to go for Declan, you've got to . . ." Eve looks up for inspiration, then says, "It's one thing to be a geek; it's another to be a proud geek, an out-there geek, a geek who says, 'Yeah, I'm here, look at me.'"

I peek at myself in the mirror, immediately look away. I suppose Eve is right. If I can't even look at myself, I can't expect Declan to.

From the floor, Syd asks, "Why does she have to do anything? The cards say it will be—why not just let it be?"

Eve says impatiently, "The cards show you one vision of the future. What you do or don't do could change everything. You can't expect everything in life to just happen to you, you have to go for it." She turns to me. "Come on, man, you're representing the despised and downtrodden of the school. You can't let them down."

"What would I have to do?" I ask suspiciously. It's not wise to give Eve total power.

"Just some shopping," she says quickly. "Maybe something with the hair." She pulls at a few strands.

I back away. "You're not chopping it off." Because Eve's crazed-scissors hairdo would send my mom into orbit.

"No," says Eve scornfully, like, *You would never have the guts for that look*. And she's right, I wouldn't. For a moment I think that maybe Eve should be the poster girl for the Eberly freaks. She's already way out there.

But she doesn't like Declan. I do. And the cards didn't say she would be with Declan. They said I would.

Am I really taking these cards seriously?

Yeah, a little bit.

And who knows? Even if the cards are wrong, maybe this is my chance to get away from blah, boring Anna for a while.

"Okay," I say. "Some shopping and maybe something with the hair."

"Yes!" shouts Eve. "The cards have spoken. It is now up to us to carry out their will. I declare this weekend Operation Freak Victory!"

That night I can't sleep. I sit on my bed and stare out the window. It's one of those hazy nights. No stars. Whatever the universe is thinking, it's not sharing.

I think: *Mrs. Rosemont, are you out there? And if you are, is this what you meant to happen?*

I look over at Mouli's crate. When Syd and Eve left, I put an old blanket in the box. Then I tried to coax him into playing by dangling a sock in front of him. He just hissed. I don't think he likes me very much.

Stupidly, I feel like everything has changed. But nothing has happened. And maybe nothing will happen. But I can't get rid of the feeling.

They're cards, Anna. They told you a little story, and that's it.

But they didn't just tell any old story. I asked a question—and they answered it.

You just think they answered it. You saw what you wanted to see.

But Eve and Sydney saw it too. And maybe Eve wanted to see it—but Syd?

Maybe Syd just got caught up in all the drama.

No matter what I come up with, there is a perfectly logical explanation for all of it. But no matter how many logical explanations I come up with . . .

I can't help feeling that this has nothing to do with logic.

FOUR

THE HIGH PRIESTESS

Wise, knowledgeable, the querent if female

The morning of the launch of Operation Freak Victory, I leap out of bed, shower, and dress in five minutes flat. I put some tuna—one can, my mom won't miss it—in Mouli's bowl, refill his water dish, then rush to the kitchen to wolf down a bowl of cornflakes before Syd and Eve arrive. Eve is getting up especially early for this. Normally on a weekend, she doesn't fall out of bed before noon.

My mom is leaning against the stove, cradling a cup of coffee in her hands. Watching me eat, she says, "I think the rule is chew before you swallow."

I mumble, "Going out with Eve and Syd," then swallow.

Mom pours herself some more coffee. "But you'll be back by four, right?"

A warning bell goes off in my head. "What's at four?"

"You're taking care of Russell tonight, remember? I have my real estate class."

I didn't remember. With the craziness of the cards, I totally forgot about my mom's class. She has it every Saturday, which—when Russell and I aren't at my dad's—means I have to babysit Fungus Toad.

This stinks. I'd imagined having the whole day to make myself over. Afterward, Syd, Eve, and I were going to go out to dinner and . . .

Then I look at my mom. She's rubbing her eyes with the heel of her hand. She looks really tired.

I say, "We'll totally be done by then."

My mom smiles, touches my head. "Thanks, kiddo. You're the best."

I smile back, hoping my mother will still think that after I tell her about Mouli. I'm going to have to soon. I've got him hidden in my closet. Litter box near clothes—not a good thing.

I'm ashamed to admit this, but I know nothing—zero, zilch, nada—about shopping. I am probably the only girl in school who still shops with her mother. But Eve and Syd are going to take me to all their favorite places. They swear the Great Geek Look can be achieved. I'm like, *Okay, fine, but can it be achieved by* me?

On the subway down to the Village, I ask them if we can go back to my place after shopping on account of Russell. Eve rages, "God, your mother treats you like a total slave."

To change the subject, Syd asks, "How's Mouli?"

I shake my head. "Still freaked out. Won't let me near him at all. I don't know why Mrs. Rosemont gave me him and not one of the other cats." Even as I say this, I feel terrible. Poor Mouli. It's not his fault he's psycho.

"What happened to the other cats?" Syd asks. Eve rolls her eyes; she is not into pets. The last living thing her parents gave her was a goldfish. She flushed it down the toilet—so it could be free in the ocean, she claimed.

Guessing, I say, "Maybe she left them to friends?"

"I wonder if we should try to find them," says Syd thoughtfully. "A lot of times people say they'll take someone's pet, then abandon it because they didn't really want it in the first place."

I'm about to say, *That's horrible* when I realize that if my mom doesn't let me keep Mouli, that's exactly what will happen to him.

"We should make sure they're okay," says Syd worriedly.

"They're *cats*," says Eve. "Can we not get all crazy and goo-goo?"

Hastily, seeing Syd's killer look, I say, "Maybe Ruben can tell us how to reach them."

"Why?" says Eve.

I remember how I imagined Mouli, Tat, and Beesley frightened and in cages in some shelter. It's an awful image. It's worth calling a few strangers to make sure it doesn't come true. But that's not something I can explain to Eve, so I don't try.

The subway lurches to a halt; the doors hiss open.

Eve says, "Shopping time."

First Eve takes us to her "all-time favorite place." This is a store called Roadkill. As we go in, I spot a fortune-teller next door. The sign says: MADAME ADORA. PALMISTRY. CRYSTALS. TAROT CARDS. For a second I wonder if I should talk to Madame Adora. If she would say, *Trust not the dark, spiky one. Make no purchases today.*

"Wow," says Syd as we walk in. "Black." Because *everything* in the store is black. Black or metal.

Eve goes directly to a pair of thigh-high boots with outrageous spikes. "Are these amazing or what?"

Syd frowns. "I don't know if I see Anna as a biker chick."

"Are you kidding? These are for me. For Anna, I'm thinking this. . . ." She holds up a pair of army pants, a studded belt, and a tank top. I can already tell, the tank top is going to show the whole world that I have an innie.

"Couldn't I do a T-shirt?" I say.

"No way. This is ideal freak warfare gear. Come on, let's try it."

I do, keeping my head down the entire time so I don't accidentally catch sight of myself in the mirror before I'm ready. When I get the nerve to peek, everything looks okay from the neck down. But the "Please don't laugh at me" expression on my face wrecks the image.

Syd and Eve reluctantly agree. "It's more something you would wear," Syd says to Eve.

Eve nods. "Let's go girlier."

Before we leave, she buys the boots. It wipes out her clothing allowance for the entire year, but Eve says it's worth it.

Next store: Ambience. Lots of color here: pink, orange, purple—all the shades you'd pick for gumballs. Everything I try on makes me look like a dorky cheerleader. As I stand in front of the mirror, wondering if this is what Declan likes, Syd says, "*Definitely* not Anna."

Eve says, "Total P&P."

I say, "Thank God."

Syd picks the next place, a store her mother takes her to for family occasion outfits. It's so Muffy, Eve refuses to go inside. All the store people wear suits and talk in whispers. They keep looking at us like we're going to steal something. Picking through a pile of sweaters, Syd admits, "These are more for church than seducing. Oh, hey"—she picks up a pretty plaid skirt—"this is kind of cool."

"With your legs, it'd look great."

She buys it.

Over lunch Syd says, "Let me get this straight. Are we going for the perfect look for Anna or something this guy Declan will like?"

I say, "Perfect look for Anna," as Eve says, "Something Declan will like."

Syd says to Eve, "It's no good if Anna doesn't like it."

"What good is it if Declan doesn't like it?"

I say, "Guys, I think I might be hopeless."

"No way," says Eve. "You must trust in the cards. Your recent past card said you had a chance for new opportunities, right? Well, what good is that if you don't make the most of it?"

Syd giggles. "You're getting really weird with those cards."

Next store: too slutty. Store after that: too cutesy. Store after that: "too friggin' hideous for words." In fact, it's so hideous, we decide we must have a Frappacino break to recover.

Next up, a mega department store. As we push through the revolving doors, Eve says, "I don't know how freak this is, but they've got everything."

Inside, I check out some shirts and wonder how these scraps of fabric are supposed to transform me into Ms. Freaky Fabulous. I glance over at Syd, who's holding a pair of striped pants to her waist. As she bends over to check them out, her curly hair bounces like red bubbles. I remember when I first met her, I thought, *Man, red hair and freckles*. It seemed like the most romantic thing. I figured that you would totally know who you were if you looked like that. If Syd died, people would get hysterical. There'd be tons of animals at her funeral. Her piano teacher would weep and say she was the most gifted student she ever had.

I glance over at Eve, who's looping several bracelets on her arm. I hope she "remembers" to take them all off. That's a little trick of hers. She doesn't think of it as stealing. She thinks of it as "redistribution of wealth." She catches me watching her, crosses her eyes, and sticks out her tongue. I laugh, she's so outrageous. I envy the way she looks, with her chopped-up hair, enormous green eyes, and big wide mouth. My mom always says Eve could be so pretty if she stopped trying to look ugly. My mom doesn't get that sometimes pretty's not the point.

Syd buys the pants. Eve walks out with a bracelet and a sample lipstick. Guess who still hasn't found anything yet?

But just as I'm about declare myself a total loser, we pass a tiny secondhand clothes store. In the window there's a long dress that's made out of lace, a crazy tie-dyed shirt, and a hat with a huge faded rose on the brim. A pair of ruby slippers sits beside a pair of battered army boots. Long strands of beads are hanging from the ceiling. It feels like the most welcoming place I've seen all day.

We go inside, and I start rifling through the clothes on the rack. Right away, like they were there waiting for me, I find a pair of dark green velvet pants. They look like someone I could be, someone I'd want to be. Holding them up, I ask Syd and Eve, "What do you think?"

Syd nods excitedly. "Wait—hold on." She pushes some shirts and sweaters aside, gets out a black turtleneck. "It's got a little hole in the sleeve, but I think it'd go great with those."

There's no real dressing room in the store, just an old curtain and a mirror, so Eve and Syd stand guard while I try on the pants and sweater. This time I can't wait to look in the mirror. When I do, I just grin. Because I finally get why people love shopping. It's like opening a beautifully wrapped package and finding yourself inside.

For a second I try to see Declan's Future Girlfriend in the mirror. I'm not sure if I do or not.

Eve checks out the clothes. "Not as freaky as I wanted, but definitely not P&P. And definitely not blah. I approve."

After that, it's like I've broken my shopper's block. I buy the pants, the sweater, a purple shirt that is a little small for me—but Eve says that's a good thing—and a chunky silver cuff. Last, I buy the hat with the rose on the brim. I'm not sure I'd ever have the nerve to wear it, but I can't bear to leave it behind, all alone and lonely in the window.

As we come out of the shop, Syd says, "Where next?"

I say, "I think we're done." Once the shopping gods have blessed you, you shouldn't be ungrateful and ask for more. Besides, I'm out of money.

"Fine," says Eve. "Now . . . hair time."

As we troop into my lobby burdened with shopping bags, I see Ruben mopping by the stairs and remember what Syd said about finding Tat and Beesley.

Setting my bags down, I say, "Hey, Ruben. You know Mrs. Rosemont's cats?"

He grins. "Sure do. How's your mother taking it?"

"Haven't quite told her yet. Do you know how to find out where Tat and Beesley went?"

He shakes his head. "I can't tell you that."

Syd comes up behind me. "Please, Ruben? We won't bother the new owners, I swear. We just want to make sure the cats are okay. Sometimes people say they'll take pets just to make the owner feel better, then they get rid of them."

Ruben bunches his mouth to the side; he knows Syd is right. "I'll think about it."

My mom is waiting at the door when we come in. Planting a big kiss on Russell's head, then on mine, she calls, "Be good, girls," and splits.

Eve turns to Russell and says, "Russell, do you know where the TV is?" He nods, picks his nose. "Can we rely on you not to electrocute yourself?" He nods again, lets his finger drift toward his mouth. But Eve slaps his hand away, saying, "Boogers can kill. Just say no."

Then she leads us all down the hall to my room and closes the door.

While Syd goes to let Mouli out of the closet, Eve places me in front of the full-length mirror. "Hair down, please."

"Please, don't make me Cousin Itt," I beg.

Eve yanks the band out of my hair and starts brushing. As she does, she says, "Come on, Anna, you have this gorgeous hair, but you never wear it down."

I check myself in the mirror, see two nervous eyes peering out from an avalanche of hair. Does Eve really think my hair is gorgeous? To me, it just looks brown.

For half an hour Eve and Syd pull my hair this way and that way. Mouli creeps out from the closet to watch us. But if he has an opinion on my hair, he keeps it to himself.

Finally, Eve looks at Syd. Syd looks at Eve. Together they say, "Cousin Itt."

Then Syd says, "Wait a sec. Sit down. Give me a brush," she says to Eve. Digging in her pocket, she pulls out some rubber bands, "What if . . . ?"

"What if what?" I trust Syd way more than Eve. But I'm not feeling very brave right now. I might as well be buck naked in Times Square with the whole world laughing at me.

Syd is pulling thin strands of my hair back and

fiddling with them. "What are you doing?" I ask, twisting to look in the mirror.

"Hold still. You'll like it, I promise."

Head down, I wait while Syd pulls and fiddles, pulls and fiddles. Then she pulls a clip out of her own hair and puts it in mine. Finally, she says, "Okay, look."

What she's done is made several braids. They're slender, almost unnoticeable, except that there are a lot of them, and they swing against the mass of my hair. Two of them are pulled back and into the clip that holds my hair off my face. It looks cool. Funky. Like me . . . but not.

I say, "Um . . ."

"Yeah?" Syd and Eve are standing behind me, watching to see how I react to my reflection.

"I think I kind of love it."

"Yes!" They're hugging me from either side when there's a huge banging on the door. Russell. Russell cannot see Mouli. He's so nuts for animals, there's no way he'd be able to keep Mouli secret from my mom. And there's no way I'm prepared to tell her just yet.

I open the door a tiny crack and say, "What?"

He looks at the door. "Why can't I come in?"

"You know the rules. What do you need, Russell?"

Just at that moment Mouli decides to get up and

stretch. I think: *No, Mouli, do not come over here. The enemy is here, Mouli. . . .*

Mouli meows. Loudly. Russell, who is dense but not deaf, says, "That's a cat."

"It is absolutely not a cat." Mouli is padding toward the door. Syd runs over to grab him, but all she does is startle him, so he bolts, managing to squeeze past me and race out into the hall.

Russell watches him go, then says to me, "You are so dead."

"A cat?"

Despite my offer to make him owner of Mouli on Wednesdays and Fridays, Russell gives my mom the good news the very next morning. Before she's had her coffee or anything. Needless to say, she is now in a fantastic mood.

From the table, I say, "I'll take care of him, you know I will."

"Me too," says Russell. He is sticking his Cheerios into his ear to see how many will fit.

My mom smiles at him. "I know you would, honey." "Would." Not "will." Not good.

"Mom, Mrs. Rosemont gave him to me. It would be totally wrong not to keep him. In some cultures it's a deadly insult to refuse a gift."

"And I'm sure in those cultures they don't give people gifts that shed and scratch up the furniture."

I don't know how to explain to my mom that Mrs. Rosemont's leaving me the cards and Mouli and my quest for unblahness are somehow connected. That I can't give him away because I was destined to have him. I don't know why, but I was.

"Besides, I have allergies," says my mom.

I'm about to say she doesn't really have allergies, she just pretends she does because she hates cats, when Mouli comes sliding into the kitchen. He pads around, then sits at my mom's feet and looks up at her. His tail twitches slightly. He really is adorable when he wants to be, this fat, orange, stripy thing. I'll scream if my mom makes me give him up.

"See, Mom?" says Russell. "He likes you."

"He likes the eggs I'm making." She looks down at him. "What's its name?"

"Mouli," I say quickly, thinking, *Once you know something's name, you can't give it away. Like, you're not strangers anymore.* That has to be a rule somewhere in the world.

"Are you going to make me sneeze, Mouli?" my mother asks, spatula in hand. Mouli just stares at her like, *Maybe.*

I look over at Russell. His eyes are wide. He's holding his breath, which is what he does when he really wants something. I smile. I can't hate him when he wants to keep Mouli so bad.

Mom points the spatula at both of us. "You promise to keep him out of my room and away from the living room as much as possible?"

We chorus, "Yes!"

"And I never, ever have to touch kitty litter?"

"Never," I say.

My mom sighs. "Welcome to the family, Mouli."

Russell yells, "Come see my room, Mouli!" and charges out of the kitchen. My mom smiles after him. Then she sits down at the table opposite me, takes a long sip of her coffee.

I poke at my cereal, trying to get it all under the milk. I know my mom is letting me keep Mouli partly because she feels guilty about working so hard and taking classes. Mouli is my reward for babysitting.

So, now that we are keeping Mouli, does this mean that tomorrow I will wear my fabulous new clothes to school and Declan will fall at my feet in a swoon of passion?

I'm not sure. Actually, it sounds kind of ridiculous when I think about it.

I say, "Mom, can I ask you a question?"

"Does it have to do with cats?" I shake my head. "Then shoot."

"Do you believe in fate?"

Startled, my mom says, "Fate?"

"Yeah, like . . . destiny. Like your life is all planned out and you can look into the future."

She shakes her head. "I'm a big believer in free will, honey. It's up to you to make your life happen. The choices you make, the actions you take . . . that's what determines things. Not some mystical force."

"Oh." I am a little disappointed that this is what my mother thinks. I mean, I can choose Declan, but who says Declan will choose me?

Then my mother says, "And I sort of believe in karma."

"What's karma?"

"It's like the energy you create by the things you do. Like if you do good things, you create good karma and that comes back to you eventually. If you put out bad karma, you'll—"

"Get zapped."

"Right." My mom smiles. "But all-controlling, powerful fate? Nuh-uh."

Okay, so my mother doesn't believe in fate.

But if that's the case, why does she read her horoscope every day?

After breakfast I'm headed back to my room to call Syd with the good news that we can keep Mouli. When I pass by the front door, I notice someone has pushed a piece of paper under it. Picking it up, I read,

> **Anna—**
> **I can't give you the addresses, but to find Beesley, call 718-555-0838. To find Tatiana, call 718-555-9467. Good luck!**
> **Ruben**

As I go by Russell's room, I see Mouli curled up on his bed. Russell is dangling a piece of string over his head, but Mouli just looks annoyed.

I think, *Okay, cat, you've got your new home. Does this mean I get Declan?*

No answer.

I go back to my room to set out my new outfit.

FIVE

EIGHT OF WANDS, SIDEWAYS

Arrows of love, arrows of jealousy

The next morning as I brush my teeth, I think, *Today is my first day as Declan's Future Girlfriend.*

Green velvet pants, check. Black turtleneck, check. Braids . . . a little messy after sleeping on them, but I *think* check.

I survey the results in the mirror. It's not as "wow" as when I saw it for the first time, but it's a vast improvement. I stare at myself, challenging the image to disappear.

The cards have spoken, I tell myself. *You must carry out the will of the cards.*

Coming out of my room, I run into my mother.

She looks at what I'm wearing and says, "Well, this is a new you."

"In a good way or a bad way?" I ask nervously.

She laughs. "Honey, it's fine. You look . . . very nice."

Fine? Very nice? Why do I feel this is Mom-speak for "hideous"?

I find Russell in the kitchen, feeding the inside of an Oreo to Mouli by letting him lick it off his finger. I say, "Russell, let's go," and he grabs his book bag.

He says, "Bye, Mouli. Have a great day. Be good. Don't barf on Mom's bed. What?" He puts his head close to Mouli's, then tells me, "He says don't worry, he'll barf on your bed."

"Go . . . ," I say, shoving him toward the door. As I follow, I turn back to Mouli and say, "What do you think? Giving fate a helping hand here or what?"

Mouli blinks. Inscrutably.

Thanks, cat. Glad I saved your life.

It's no small thing to appear at school with a totally different look. At Eberly, people will stomp you if you try to be something you're not—or something they think you shouldn't try to be. People got hysterical when Susie Chen danced hip-hop at Spring Fling. They tortured Liza Kettle when she became a redhead and tried to claim that her hair had just changed over the summer. And when Dennis Fink, who has really bad B.O., ran for class president, a lot of kids wrote in *Nobody* on the ballot, just to show him what they thought of him daring to think he might be acceptable.

By the time I get to school, I am a nervous wreck. The second I see Eve, I whisper, "Are you sure I look okay?"

Eve stares at me. "What's wrong with you? You look great."

I glance down at myself, wishing I was in plain old jeans and a sweater like always. Maybe I can just wear my coat everywhere.

Eve must guess what I'm thinking because she says, "The only way you can screw this up is by acting all 'Oh, don't look, don't look.'" She gives me a shove. "Go. Bring down your prey."

As I head to class, I try to remind myself that the cards are behind me, that I am the champion of the Eberly freaks, and even Eve thinks I look good.

But then I remember Zoe's World. How she told everyone about my humiliating encounter with Declan. Whenever Zoe puts something juicy on the site, people talk about it for days.

Oh, my God, are they talking about me?

Did you see Zoe's World's? ChorusGrl is her, right?
God, she likes Declan? How pathetic!
And she thinks she'll get him in that? Sad, sad, sad . . .

In English, Ms. Taramini writes a word on the board: *hubris.* She explains that it has to do with pride and arrogance, thinking you're more powerful than you are. She says Oedipus had hubris in thinking he could change his destiny and that's partly why the gods punished him. I have the awful feeling she's talking about me.

I make it to lunch without anyone laughing in my face. I swear I hear a few people humming "The Water Is Wide," but that could be just my imagination.

No one says I look horrible.

No one says I look great, either.

And I still have the biggest test of all: the lunchroom. If you want to see who's in and who's not at Eberly, check out the cafeteria. The lowliest sit in the Lowest Circle, as in hell, either near the entrance, where they get jostled by everyone coming in, or in the back near the vending machines. The über-cool have a space all to themselves, called the Subzero Zone. If you're not part of their crowd, you're not allowed to sit there. Well, you can, but you'll get butter pats thrown at you.

Tray tipping is big in the lunchroom. If the über-cools want to let you know you're out, that's usually how it starts. I am going to be really pissed if someone tips a tray on my new pants.

As we head downstairs to lunch, Eve says, "Any sign of His Dudeliness yet?"

I shake my head. Eve frowns; because if someone's your destiny, shouldn't you have seen them by now?

Then she says, "Come on, I bet we find him in the cafeteria."

Waiting on line, I scan the room for Declan. Declan always eats the same thing for lunch: noodles with ketchup. It used to seem like the last word in retarded, and it made a real mess when guys like Chris Abernathy tipped his tray. "Oh, hey, sorry, Ark-Ark." Now everyone eats it. Even Elissa Maxwell's scarfing egg noodles smothered in Heinz.

But I don't see him. I look at the girls sitting in Subzero. Elissa's there, of course, and Alexa with dim Marnie. P&P is right. They're like a cult of pretty people, with a mandate from the heavens: Thou shalt congregate only with those of perfect hair and perfect bodies and inane giggles. And thou shalt mate with only those of thine own kind. The hot, the cool, the seriously amazing. I wonder if Declan would need divine dispensation to date me.

Eve nudges me, says, "I think there's a decent seat over there." I look and see that in order to get there, we have to pass by Subzero. I wish we didn't. The P&Ps think it's their job to approve everyone's clothes; if they don't like what you're wearing, believe me, they let you know it. As we pass, I think to myself, *Ignore them. Don't let them get to you.*

Then, almost by accident, I turn and see Alexa staring at me. Our eyes meet, and she raises her eyebrow. Then she pulls her head back, like she wants to get the full view . . . and sneers.

There's no other word for it. Her forehead wrinkles, her mouth twists up in this ugly way, then she whispers to Marnie—just loud enough so I can hear— "I thought Halloween wasn't for another month."

In that moment I hate Alexa Roth more than I thought it was possible to hate any one human being. Red-faced with rage and embarrassment, I swing right, wanting to get away from Subzero as fast as possible . . .

And walk straight into Declan.

Correction: straight into Declan's tray. Which flips up, depositing his lunch all over his feet.

I can't believe it. I have just tipped Declan Kelso's tray.

Declan can't believe it either. He's staring down at his

noodles and ketchup like he expects them to leap back onto the plate, for the tray to jump back into his arms. There's noodles on his shoes, ketchup on my pants.

I say, "I am so sorry."

But I don't think he hears me because the entire lunchroom is cracking up.

"You didn't mean it," Eve says in the bathroom as I wash ketchup out of my pants.

"Yeah, I'm sure that matters to him." I scrub my cuff with a paper towel. "I'm sure that right now he's thinking, 'I know Anna didn't mean it. I'll ask her out tomorrow.'"

"At least you got his attention," says Eve. "And Alexa, man—what a cow. That's how you know you look good. Miss Diva Wannabe saw you and freaked."

I look at my pants. "Well, at least she didn't tip Declan's tray."

As if my day weren't bad enough, after lunch I have gym. Someday I want to meet the sicko who invented dodgeball. How is this a fun game? Throw balls at people—really hard. Try to hit their bare skin, so it stings. See if you can hit someone in the head without the teacher noticing. Maybe you can cause brain damage! Twenty points!

And what malevolent god decided I should have to play dodgeball with Chris Abernathy and Kyle Fletcher? Chris and Kyle love dodgeball. What do they love about it? Hurling the ball really hard at girls' chests. And Mr. Petrie, the teacher, lets them get away with it, every single time.

Not only do I have Chris and Kyle in my gym class, I also have Nelson Kobliner. Nelson is frightening walking down the hall. With a ball in his hand, he's terrifying. He throws seriously hard and is never afraid to run right up to the line.

On dodgeball days I try to get out—and stay out—as much as possible.

Only because stupid Anna thought she was destined to be Declan Kelso's girlfriend, her hair is in braids, not back in a ponytail. And stupid Anna did not bring an elasto-thingy so she could put her hair back. So Anna can't see because her hair is in her face. Chris, Kyle, or Nelson could be throwing a ball directly at me, and I wouldn't have a clue until I woke up in the hospital.

I inch up to the line, hoping someone nice will hit me out, but not too hard. Nelson is right up there, of course, powering the ball across the gym like a manic King Kong. He throws it so hard, it slams against the back wall and bounces right back to his side. Last year he gave Terry Peterson a bloody nose, even though there's a rule against throwing the ball at someone's head.

I do not want to be in the way of the next ball thrown by Nelson Kobliner. As I edge away, I feel something roll against my feet. A ball. Putrid Petrie yells, "Come on, Anna, let's go."

I sigh, pick up the ball. Pushing my hair out of my eyes, I think, *Okay, Mr. Petrie. You're so hot on bloodshed? I am going to throw this ball so hard, it's going through the wall.*

I throw my arm back. Swing it around. Just as I let go, my hair falls into my face. The next thing I hear is a scream. I pull my hair back and see Nelson Kobliner holding his cheek. It is bright flaming red.

I have hit the school psycho. I am a dead woman. Any second now, I'll get a revenge ball right in the face. All around, kids are staring, wondering what Nelson will do. Chris and Kyle are cracking up. *Look, Kobliner got creamed by a girl!*

I stammer, "I'm sorry, I'm really, really sorry. . . ."

Nelson says, "No . . ." *No, you don't get to apologize for this. You must feel the pain.*

He raises his other hand. This is it. I put my hands over my face.

Then I hear, "It's o-okay."

Surprised, I take my hands down. Nelson's looking at me, puzzled. Like he can't figure out why I'm so scared of him.

I wonder: *Why am I so scared of him?*

Petrie yells, "Anna, you're out! No throwing in the face!"

As I head to the sidelines, I look back at Nelson. He's still watching me, passing the ball from hand to hand. Halfheartedly, he tosses it to the other side, but it doesn't hit anyone.

I think, *He was never going to throw that ball at you. He knew you hit him by accident.*

I watch as Chris hurls a ball straight at Kelly Dunphy's butt. Nelson never does that, throws hard at girls out of meanness.

But I forgot that. And I treated him like a freak.

I feel like a total creep.

So, let's see. On my first day as Declan's Future Girlfriend, I have been insulted by one of the most powerful girls in school. I attracted the attention of my loved one by humiliating him. And I hurt a major freak's feelings. Way to go, Anna.

Why did I ever think I could look okay? How could I ever have imagined that Declan could be into me? Why didn't I just leave it all alone?

When I get home, I am tossing those stupid cards in the garbage.

Finally, for my last class of the day, I have chorus. I do like chorus, even if it is for losers. I like singing with a big group of people who can drown out my mistakes and let me think I'm better than I really am. I'm an alto, which is code for "not great singer." There are seven altos in the chorus, whereas there are only three sopranos: Jackie, Lara, and Chloe. They pretend to be friends and all kissy-kissy, but, boy, watch out when solos get handed out.

There is one really good alto singer, and that's Bridget Halsey. But only I know how great she is, and that's because I sit next to her. Bridget is the shyest person I know. Everyone finds a way to survive Eberly. Eve by acting obnoxious, me by . . . well, I don't know if I have a way. But Bridget's way is to disappear. All of her clothes are way baggy; she sits slumped like she's hoping you'll mistake her for a pile of laundry—which most people do. Her hair is usually in her face, and when it isn't, Bridget has her hands there instead. When she first joined chorus, it took her weeks to say anything more than hi to me. But once she figured out I wasn't going to torture her, she relaxed. I always try to find something nice to say to her, sort of build up her confidence a little.

Another thing about Bridget, and the reason she wears such big clothes, is that she has the largest chest in the entire eighth grade and she's totally embarrassed by it.

As I come into the music room, Mr. Courtney shouts, "Whoa, sixties flashback! Peace and purple haze, baby." He starts banging out a Beatles song on the piano. Everyone giggles. Even my fellow altos. Thanks, guys, thanks a lot. As I scuttle to my seat, Bridget smiles hi. If anyone knows what it's like to feel conspicuous, Bridget does.

I'm about to say I like her shoes when Mr. Courtney starts singing, "'I get high with a little help from my friends . . .' Don't get high, people, just say no. Hey, speaking of friends, are we all here?" He looks around. "We're not all here. Where the heck is this guy . . . ?"

I don't get what Mr. Courtney is talking about. To me, it looks like we are all here.

Mr. Courtney starts singing, "'He's a real nowhere man . . .' Oh, hey, here he is. Not on time, but it's your first class, we'll forgive you. Second class, we kill you. Ladies, gentlemen, tenors, I introduce my newest recruit, Declan Kelso. Declan, you look like a bass to me. Why don't you go stand over there? Yeah, behind Anna, Miss Lucy in the Sky with Diamonds. Anna, give the boy some music from that pile over there."

I do, not quite managing to meet Declan's eye. But as he takes the folder, I look up to see him smiling.

In a soft voice he says, "Hey."

So, we have to ask ourselves—why is GG suddenly feeling so *musical*? I mean, who joins chorus except for the possibly talented and the positively pathetic? Could it be he has a deep, hidden desire to sing? Or can it be that GG doesn't want a career in music as much he wants a certain girl *in* the chorus?

"No way."

That's the first thing Syd says when I tell her that Declan joined chorus. And the second. And the third. She just keeps saying it. "No way."

Then she says, "You think the cards . . . like, made it happen?"

"The cards predicted it," says Eve. We're sitting in Café 96, this place where we go in between Eve's street and our street. Eve always gets espresso. I'm not sure she actually likes it, but she says it's bitter, like her. "Still, I can't believe he joined chorus, dude. That is a serious sacrifice."

"We don't actually know he joined for me," I say to be fair.

"Are you kidding? After Courtney exposed you as a chorus type right in front of him? And Zoe's World called you 'ChorusGrl'? He totally joined because of you." She sips her espresso.

I wonder if Eve remembers how Zoe said I should dump her as a friend. I'm about to point out that Zoe doesn't always know what she's talking about when Eve says, "Besides, the cards said it would happen. So . . . now it's happening."

We're leaving the café when Syd says, "Hey, guys, remember those phone numbers Ruben gave Anna? For the cats?"

I nod. "Yeah?"

Syd looks embarrassed. "I called one of them."

I can't believe it. Syd is incredible. "Which one?"

"The woman who took Beesley. She lives in Queens. She said we could come see him next weekend if we wanted to. Or even this weekend."

"This weekend we're at my dad's," I say. "But definitely next weekend."

In some ways, Russell and I are luckier than a lot of kids with divorced parents. Our dad lives just across the park and we can see him pretty much any time we want. Plus, we spend every other weekend with him, which is great. But on weekends where you have something you'd rather be doing—like rescuing a cat with your friends—it can be a bit of a drag. But I'd never, ever let my dad know that.

He meets us at the door with a big "Russell Hustle! Anna Banana!"

Before we left, Mom gave me a big envelope marked *For Dad*—containing things like book reports and holiday brochures. Now I pull it out of my bag and hand it to my dad, who says, "Thank you very much. Anything that requires my immediate attention?"

"I did a paper on bugs!" shouts Russell.

"That sounds like it requires immediate attention."

I set the table while my dad reads Russell's bug report at the kitchen table. Russell is kneeling in a chair. Every so often, he says something like, "Did you get to the part where I talk about their stomachs?" And my dad laughs and says, "Not there yet. Can't wait."

Then he takes out an essay I did on DNA. But before he has a chance to start it, he says, "Chicken's ready. Eatin' time," and sets it aside.

We sit down. Russell says, "Dad, Dad, did you get my picture? The one I sent you of Mouli?"

My dad nods solemnly. "I did get it." He looks at me. "How'd you talk your mom into a cat?"

I know Dad doesn't mean this as a knock on my mom; everyone knows she's not crazy about pets. But I feel like if I tell him how Russell and I had to beg, it'll seem like I'm complaining, that she's this awful, cold person. I wonder if he wants me to say: *Oh, man, I wish you'd been there.* . . . This happens sometimes. My dad asks me questions and because I'm not sure what he's really asking, I'm not sure what to say.

Then Russell yells, "Dad, this sauce needs more *bugs*!" and I'm off the hook.

After dinner Russell takes his bath while I help Dad wash the dishes. As we do, I think about Declan. I'm not sure what the cards want me to do now. Yeah, Declan joined chorus, but what does that mean? Did fate put him in chorus so I could talk to him? Or is Declan waiting for a chance to ask me out? If I do nothing, will something happen anyway?

Stacking up the plates on the table, I say, "Dad? Do you believe in fate?"

My dad stares at me. "Why do you ask?"

"It's a school project," I lie. "About free will and destiny and whether we have any choice in what happens to us."

"You *always* have a choice," he says.

"But we don't control everything. I could choose something and still not get what I want."

He nods. "No, absolutely true." For a weird moment I feel like he's thinking of my mom. "Nothing controls everything, Anna. Key in the mix, I would say, are other people."

I think. "Like, if you like a guy and he doesn't like you back, then you're not fated to be together."

My dad peers at me. "Say, for example . . . ?"

"Right."

He thinks for a moment. "If he doesn't like you, then it seems less likely that you'll be together. But maybe this 'guy' will come to his senses and realize he's stupid not to like you."

"Because you *were* actually fated to be together."

"No, because guys can be pretty dense." He rinses off a plate and sets it in the drying rack. "Any reason we're talking about guys?"

I shake my head. One thing I absolutely believe: Telling either of my parents about Declan and the cards will severely disrupt any cosmic energies that might bring me and Declan together. But it sounds like my dad doesn't believe in things like cards that predict the future. Which, I have to say, is a bummer.

Then Dad says, "Just an observation, but a lot of times guys are more scared of talking to girls than you might think. It can be a huge relief if, say, a girl starts the conversation."

"Really?"

He nods. "As I say, just an observation."

✸

What my dad says makes sense. After all, I did tip Declan's tray, and that's not the best way to show someone you like them. So it's up to me to make the next move. Only how? I am not one of those people who can just go up to someone and start talking.

And, it seems, neither is Declan. A week goes by, and he doesn't say a single word to me. In chorus I try to catch his eye. All I ever catch is Jackie, Lara, and Chloe doing the exact same thing. No wonder Declan never looks up from his music.

Maybe Eve's right. Maybe I should give him a bottle of ketchup. Over the weekend she says, "You guys haven't even spoken yet? I figured you'd be engaged by now." I feel like I am letting her down. Not to mention the cards and every unpopular girl at Eberly.

The next week, though, I get an idea. Because chorus is the last class of the day and there's a row of lockers outside the practice room, you usually get stuck in the crowd as you try to leave. All I have to do is get stuck in the crowd in the same place as Declan.

On Thursday, when Mr. Courtney says, "All right, people, that's it," I am out of my seat like a shot. My plan is to get out quick, then wait by the door for Declan. I saw Lara try to do this last week. But she blew it by sweeping her hair back before she spoke. By the time her hair was perfect, Declan was long gone.

I get out to the hallway pretty quickly. It's packed with kids getting their stuff to go home, and I have to fight to keep my place by the door. Bridget, who's standing next to me, folds her arms tightly against her chest so she doesn't get elbowed and plows through the crowd.

Then I see Alexa coming in from the stairwell. This makes no sense. Alexa's locker is on the third floor. There is no reason for her to be down here, unless she's trying to run into . . .

Declan. Who is coming out of the practice room right now. I pivot, land in front of him. "Hey, Declan!"

To my relief, he smiles. "Hey, Anna."

"I wanted to say I'm sorry about the tray thing. It was a total accident."

He looks startled, and I wonder for a minute if he even remembers. Then he says, "No, I was a jerk, I swung right into you. I thought . . . I thought you were probably really pissed at me."

"Really?" He nods, and for a moment everything is absolutely perfect—until he looks up over the crowd and says, "Oh, hey, sorry, I . . . I got to . . . See you."

And then he disappears. I can barely see him through the crowd, but I can see enough to know where he's going.

He's headed straight toward Alexa.

"You gotta give her credit," says Eve. "Picking him off after class is not dumb."

The subway train swerves. Grabbing the pole, Syd says, "Maybe it had nothing to do with her. Maybe he had to go to the bathroom."

Before I have a chance to point out there are no bathrooms on the basement floor, the train comes out of the tunnel, and all of a sudden, we're riding high over Queens. I have never been to Queens before. I'm a little nervous of what it'll be like.

We are going to meet Beesley's new mom, Mrs. Sylvia Friedman. I'm glad because I need something to take my mind off Declan. As the train curves on the elevated track, you can see Manhattan sprawled behind us. Everywhere you look, it's rooftops and highways. We don't have any elevated trains in Manhattan. This is like riding a roller coaster through the city.

From the subway, you have to walk three long blocks to get to Mrs. Friedman's building. The streets are crowded with people from what looks like every country on the planet. I hear, like, five different languages being spoken. There's a woman in a gorgeous colored sari pushing a baby carriage, a guy speaking Spanish into a cell phone, and an elderly Asian woman inching a shopping cart down the street. Two girls are laughing on the corner; when one of them says, "Yeah, I couldn't believe it," I hear she has an Irish accent. For a second I just stare at all the life on these streets, then Eve pulls me along.

When we get to Mrs. Friedman's building, Syd takes out a piece of paper. "It's apartment thirty-one." She looks at me. "You buzz."

I'm too nervous. "No, you."

Eve reaches over my shoulder, pushes the buzzer. After a second we hear, "Hello?"

"It's us," I blurt out, then think, *Duh, who's us?* "Mrs. Rosemont's friends? The cat?"

We wait a second, then hear, "Oh, yes," and a long buzz as we're let in.

"Well! I am very glad to see you girls. Come in, come in, come in."

Mrs. Friedman is tiny, and she moves as fast as she talks. If she didn't have white hair and wrinkles, you'd never know she was an old person. One by one, we step over the threshold into Mrs. Friedman's apartment, then follow her down a narrow hallway to a beautiful, bright living room. "I apologize for the mess," she says. "It seems like I'm doing a hundred and one things these days. I guess that's what happens when you retire." She grins. "Sit, sit, sit."

I wonder: *Is it because there are three of us that she says everything three times?*

"So, how did you young ladies know my friend Etta?"

For a second I don't know who she's talking about. Then I realize, *Oh, Etta.* That's Mrs. Rosemont's first name. Etta Rosemont. That's . . . who she was.

I say, "We fed her cats." But that doesn't sound like enough, so I add, "And we were her neighbors. Well, Syd and I were." I point to Syd, who's looking for Beesley while trying not to look like she's looking.

But Mrs. Friedman has pretty sharp eyes. "You won't find him in here, darling. Poor thing's been hiding under my desk in my bedroom since I got him. Why don't you see if you can get him to come out?"

Syd sprints toward the bedroom. Mrs. Friedman says, "I think the cat is too old to make such a big change. New place, new person. Still, when Etta left him to me, what could I say?"

"How did you know her?" asks Eve.

"We worked together in the union," says Mrs. Friedman. She must see we don't know what that means, because she smiles. "Organizing factory workers, farm laborers. Making sure their rights are protected. Power in numbers, darling."

I nod like I get it. But all the while I'm thinking, *Unions?* I don't know what I thought Mrs. Rosemont did, but I thought it was something . . . quieter. Teaching piano or something.

Syd comes in carrying Beesley and talking to him in a low, soothing voice. His eyes are very wide, and his paw is up on her shoulder like he might leap away any minute.

"Look at you, the miracle worker," says Mrs. Friedman.

"Syd's amazing with animals," says Eve.

Mrs. Friedman nods. "Some people have that gift. Me, I don't have that gift."

Syd looks up shyly. "If you're too busy for a pet, I could take him, Mrs. Friedman. Then at least he could be in his old building."

Mrs. Friedman looks thoughtful. "To be honest, I think he might like that. I think Etta gave him to me because she thought I needed company. But I'm not like she was. I like my company two-legged—no offense, Beesley."

Syd looks hopeful. "So, you wouldn't mind?"

"If it's okay with you and your parents, darling, I think it would be wonderful."

Syd thinks it'll be okay with her parents, so we decide to take Beesley now. As we leave, it feels strange that this is the only time I'll ever see Mrs. Friedman. In a weird way, it's like saying good-bye to Mrs.

Rosemont again. While Eve and Syd ring for the elevator, I hesitate by the door, not knowing what to say.

Mrs. Friedman reaches up and gives me a hug. "Thank you for being a friend to Etta." She stands back, peers at my face. "Don't worry about everything so much. It'll be fine. You'll see."

Which is exactly what Mrs. Rosemont used to say to me. For a moment I'm so shocked, I don't know what to say. Then I give Mrs. Friedman a kiss on the cheek and go to join Eve and Syd—and Beesley.

On the subway ride home, Eve asks Syd, "What are you going to tell your parents?"

"They said I could get another cat after Widget died." Syd looks lovingly at Beesley's carrier, which she's holding on her lap. "So here he is, my new cat."

"He's a little old," says Eve. "I mean, you might not . . ."

She doesn't say the rest, but she doesn't have to, because I'm thinking the same thing. Syd fell apart when they put Widget to sleep. It took her a long time to get over it. Since Beesley's thirteen, you have to wonder how soon she'll have to go through all that again—and if she can take it.

"I don't care," says Syd stubbornly. "What—just 'cause Beesley's old means he doesn't get to live the rest of his life with someone who cares about him?" She looks defiantly at us.

I say to the carrier, "You're one lucky cat, Beesley. I hope you know that."

As we get off the train, Eve says, "Back to Declan. I have a theory. The guy was a total nerdopolis. Now, all of a sudden, every girl in school wants him. Heady stuff for a former geek. Right now he's caught up in the whole nice girl versus hot girl thing, and that's just death."

Nice girl—me and the High Priestess. Intelligent, nice—and boring. I remember the reading, how I was crossed with the Eight of Wands. Thinking of how Declan bounded through the crowd to get to Alexa, I feel the arrows of jealousy, right in the heart.

Eve goes on, "We need an event, something out of school, where you can show you're not just Ms. Nice. Something like . . ."—she points—"Halloween!"

I say, "But they're not having the dance this year."

Eve says excitedly, "But Marnie Stonor is throwing a party at her house. And I bet her good bud Alexa told her to because she wants to make her move on Declan there. Only picture it this way: At the last moment you show up, dressed in some fabulous costume. Declan cannot believe his eyes. It's victory for the freaks and a crushing blow for the P&Ps!"

SIX

SIX OF CUPS, UPSIDE DOWN
New opportunities or failed plans

When Ms. Kenworthy told us that the traditional Halloween dance was going to be replaced by a charity drive for the homeless, we were like, *Are you insane?* Because as lame as the Halloween dance is, everyone likes to show off their costumes and see who sneaks off to neck in the stairwell. People said the reason they canceled the dance this year was because they caught Peter Caminiti and Debbie Fowler all tangled up with each other last year. Peter tried to pretend they'd come as Siamese twins connected by the tongue, but nobody believed him.

The teachers keep telling us, "But you're getting the Turkey Trot at the Harvest Festival instead!" Big whoop. You're supposed to do wicked things on Halloween. Thanksgiving, you're supposed to . . . give thanks.

So everyone was furious until Marnie Stonor came up with the idea of having a Halloween party at her house. Suddenly, everyone saw that having a free pass to be out of the house—*Hey, Mom and Dad, I'm collecting for charity, you* can't *give me a curfew*—wasn't actually the worst thing in the world. So the unofficial plan is after you collect for charity, you go straight to a store, spend it on stuff for the party, and go to Marnie's house. Then you tell your parents you couldn't get anyone to donate and make them cough up ten bucks.

Now everyone's excited again. Especially Ms. Kenworthy, because people are signing up like mad to collect money for the homeless and she thinks it's this wonderful display of humanitarian spirit. What she doesn't realize is that the sign-up sheet is the unofficial guest list for the party. As I put my name down, I check to make sure Declan is coming. His name's on the list—only the handwriting looks suspic·ously like Alexa's.

Then I notice that Nelson put his name down too. But someone's crossed it off and written, *Don't bother.* Sometimes I think you can't blame people in this school for acting psycho, the way some of them get treated.

I scribble over the *Don't bother*, hope Nelson never saw it.

Naturally, with Declan coming, all the girls are going crazy figuring out their costumes. The rumor is that Alexa is going as her Dalmatian, Pippa, in a white bodysuit with spots. Elissa is renting her costume from someplace, and Lara is going as a whacked-out action babe. Meanwhile, I haven't got the first clue what I'm going to wear. This afternoon Syd, Eve, and I are getting together at Syd's house to figure it out. Eve told me to bring the cards; I don't know why. What are they going to say? *You must dress as a penguin— oh, and forget about Declan. We got that wrong, sorry.*

I can't believe how great Beesley looks. At Mrs. Friedman's house, he looked like someone had shrunk him in the hot water cycle. Now he looks full and happy. Even his stripes look brighter. You have to pick him up carefully because he has a touch of arthritis. But you can tell he's in heaven living with Syd.

"He looks terrific," I tell her, feeling a little sad that Mouli never wants to curl up in my lap. We've had him for more than a month, and he still acts like I don't exist.

"Yeah," says Syd. "My mom calls him a distinguished old gent."

Eve says, "Meeting called to order. Topic under discussion: Halloween." Stuffing popcorn in her mouth, she says to Syd, "You're coming with us that night, right?"

"Definitely," says Syd. "But do you mind if I collect for the Wildlife Federation instead?"

I say, "What are you going as?"

"A fur coat," says Syd. "I'm going to get all these fake fur pieces, glue them on to some old clothes, and splatter red paint on them."

I nod. "Gross but effective. Eve?"

"I'm going as Death. I'm going to borrow one of my dad's suits, wear dark glasses . . ."

Syd asks, "How will people know you're Death and not a businessman?"

"You know those stickers they have at parent-teacher conference night? 'Hello, My Name Is . . .'? Mine will be 'Hello, My Name Is Death.'"

"That's pretty cool," says Syd admiringly.

"It is," I say, thinking there's two good ideas gone. Not that I would ever be Death or a fur coat, but now I have to be something as good as Death and a fur coat.

"I thought you'd do Death like the tarot cards," says Syd. "The skeleton riding on a horse."

Eve raises her finger, says, "Ah, since you mention the cards . . ." She holds her hand out, and I get the cards from my bag and pass them to her. Picking through the deck, she says, "I figured since the cards said you would get your true love, they should help you out with a costume. So here is what you will be wearing for Halloween . . ."

She holds up a card. It's the High Priestess, the card that was supposed to represent me in the reading. *Wisdom, knowledge, secrecy.*

I look. The High Priestess is wearing some very ugly clothes. She's got this weird hat that looks like a crystal ball with two wings coming out of the sides. It screams, *Dork!*

Thankfully, Sydney says, "How can she make a costume out of that? It's hideous."

"A tarot card is a good idea, though," I say quickly. "What else is there?"

We start looking through the cards. Syd holds up the Empress, who has this neat crown made of stars. "How about her?"

"What's the definition?" asks Eve. "You don't want to go as Dumb Slut of the Universe."

Syd checks the book. "Fruitfulness . . ." She grins. "Action. Oh, also ignorance and doubt."

"Forget it," I say. Then I spot another card, someone holding a pole with a pouch on the end, like they're running away. It looks like what Eric Davis wore to play Romeo in the senior play last year: a tunic, boots, and tights.

I hold it up. "This could be cute and easy to make."

Eve looks at it. "The Fool?"

Syd reads the definition. "'Someone starting out on a journey, recklessness, exuberance. Also folly.'" She points to the card. "I mean, look, he's about to step off a cliff."

But I'm thinking of recklessness and exuberance. I want to be reckless. I want to do what no one would expect—even if it means stepping off the occasional cliff. I don't want to be worried and shy all the time.

"That's it," I say. "That's what I'll be."

If I had any doubts that the Fool was the perfect costume, they vanish when I start putting the actual outfit together. I have a pair of boots and a pair of red tights. A mop handle and some clothes tied up in one of my mom's scarves will do for the pouch. In my closet there's an old beret; if I sew some colorful fabric on to it, it'll look like the Fool's cap.

Now all I need is the tunic. I'm thinking I'll use a too-big shirt and belt it in, so I look in my closet for something suitable. But none of my shirts are big enough—or nice enough.

I'm sitting on the floor of my room, looking at all my clothes on the floor, when Mouli suddenly jumps up and runs out into the hallway. Listening to the light thud of his paws, I can tell he's headed toward my mother's room—an absolute no-no. I follow him, shutting the door to my mom's room just in time. I tell Mouli, "Hey, just because she's not there now doesn't mean she won't figure out who's been sleeping on her bed."

Mouli meows, his tail twitching in frustration. "You want to see inside her room?" I ask him. "I promise you, it's no big deal." I open the door and show him. "See? You're not missing anything."

But when I start to close the door, I see it: a bright silk shirt lying on my mother's chair. It's beautiful, white and gold and very ornate.

It's the Fool's tunic.

Making sure Mouli is outside, I go in my mom's room and shut the door. Carefully, I lift the shirt and slide it over my head. It drops to right above my knee, with plenty of room to belt it in. I don't even have to look in the mirror to know it's fabulous.

Now all I have to do is get my mom to let me wear it.

I come out to see Mouli right outside the room, like he's been waiting for me.

"Tell me you didn't mean that to happen," I say to him.

He blinks. Inscrutably.

Generally, if I want something from my mom, it's best to wait until after dinner. Bombarding her the second she gets home can work, but it can also backfire later when she says, "Wait a minute, I said yes to what?"

So I don't ask the minute she gets home. Instead, I set the table without being asked, clear without being asked, and load up the dishwasher without being asked. My mom smiles and says, "Thanks, honey. I'll be in a coma in the living room if you need me."

When the kitchen is spotless, I go into the living room, where she's watching a news program. Sitting down next to her, I say, "Ma, can I ask you a big favor?"

"Sure, honey," she says. "And then I'll ask *you* a big favor."

"You go first," I say, thinking that she can't say no to mine if I say yes to hers.

"No, you asked first, go ahead."

I wait till the commercial, then say, "You know that white and gold shirt you have?"

My mom smiles. "That very expensive white and gold shirt I have, yes."

"Well, if I promise that nothing will happen to it—absolutely nothing—can I borrow it for Halloween?" I can tell my mom is about to say no, so I keep talking. "It's just that it's perfect for my costume, and I won't find or be able to make anything half as good, and I promise I will not let a thing happen to it." I throw in my last-ditch promise: "I'll even pay for the cleaning."

My mom hesitates. "You promise you won't let anything get on it?"

"I promise."

"It's yours."

I shriek and jump up to hug her. Sometimes my mom can be very cool. Not often, but sometimes.

When I let her go, she says, "Okay, here's my favor."

"Anything, anything . . ."

"I have my class that night, right? And you'll be staying over at your dad's, but here's the thing . . ." I nod. "I need you to take Russell and his friend Teddy trick-or-treating."

I think. Trick-or-treating in our building starts at seven. And it can go on for hours because a lot of people give out candy. Marnie's party starts at seven. Ergo . . .

Ergo, I am totally screwed.

I say, "Can't Dad take him?"

"Your dad's already getting off early from work as it is, sweetie. I told him you'd be at his house by nine."

I groan. Getting Russell to Dad's house by nine means there's no way can I get to Marnie's party before nine thirty. Alexa will spend hours with Declan, and I'll have no shot at all.

I try, "Just, there's this party and—"

"I know, honey, I know."

I'm like, *What do you know? I never even told you about the stupid party. You have no clue how important this is to me—and what's worse, you don't even care.*

My mom says, "If there was another way to do this . . ."

I want to say, *Well, actually, Mom, there is another way to do this. There are several ways. Russell could not go trick-or-treating. Or you could skip your stupid class. Or Dad could say,* Sorry, I'm not cooking tonight. *But that's not going to happen because the way it works around here is that you all get everything you want, because Anna doesn't have a life. So she's always around to do the stuff other people don't want to. Like taking stupid Fungus Toad Russell trick-or-treating!*

Then I hear "Mom?" and look up to see Russell standing at the entrance to the living room. He's in his pajamas, and he's holding Bruce, his stuffed bear that he named after Bruce Springsteen, this singer my mom likes. Russell's always had a Bruce; I think this is Bruce the Third. Not many seven-year-olds would be caught dead with a stuffed animal, but Russell is very loyal. He's weird that way. Also kind of sweet that way.

He says to my mom, "Can I ask Anna now?"

My mom smiles crookedly. "Well, you can try."

I give the coffee table a kick. "Yes, I'll take you trick-or-treating, Russell."

Mom jumps in with, "Say thank you, Russell."

"Thank you," says Russell promptly, then whispers to my mom like I can't hear, "But that's not what I wanted to ask her."

"What did you want to ask me?" I say suspiciously.

His finger disappears up his nostril. "Well, you know how—"

"Don't ask me things when you're picking your nose."

"Oh, sorry." He clutches Bruce tighter. "You know how for Halloween I'm going as a wizard?"

I sigh. "Yes."

Russell swallows. "Well, wizards have cats, like familiars, you know? And so I wanted to know if I could take Mouli with me. As my familiar. But Mom said I had to ask you, on account of he's your cat." As he says this, he looks sad; he really loves Mouli.

I pat the couch next to me, and Russell scrambles up between me and Mom. I say, "Will you take him in the carrier?"

Russell nods fervently. Several times.

"Will you not be a goober and let him out while we're trick-or-treating?"

Very slowly, Russell shakes his head.

"Can I hold Bruce for a sec?"

Russell hesitates, then hands Bruce over to me. I rest my chin on top of his furry head, smell peanut butter and grape juice. I wish I still thought animals like Bruce could protect you from everything sad or bad. Who knows, maybe they can. Maybe I need a Bruce.

Into Bruce's fur I say, "Then you can take Mouli."

The next day I have to tell Eve that I might be a little late for Marnie's party. Needless to say, she doesn't take it well.

"Your mom, man," she fumes. "You need to remind her you have a life."

"I know, but it's a big thing to Russell."

"What about you and Declan? That's a big thing to you, right? You can't leave him alone with Ms. Bowwow for too long." She sighs. "I guess Syd and me'll go early, keep an eye on them. But don't take forever, okay?"

I feel terrible. Me getting together with Declan is almost as big a thing for Eve as it is for me. If it doesn't happen, I'll have totally let her down. But if I don't take Russell trick-or-treating, that's letting *him* down, and I can't do that, either. It's like no matter what I do, I'm screwing someone up.

Just once, I'd like to be one of those people who gets everything they want because they don't care about anyone but themselves. Not for forever, but every once in a while would be nice.

What makes this situation even more dire is that there's no guarantee Declan will look at me and say, *You are the woman of my dreams.* He could be thinking he's hooking up with Alexa for all I know.

I'm totally bummed as I head to chorus. Maybe everyone else is too, because it's one of those days where nothing goes right. Wrong notes, wrong entrances, wrong words. Fifteen minutes into class, Mr. Courtney is screaming. He hurls an eraser at the basses, then tells the rest of us to take a break while he decides if he has to "fire" all of them.

Sitting next to me, Bridget cringes. She hates it when Courtney goes mental—even though he never yells at her.

In my head I count up the number of apartments we have to hit on Halloween, trying to figure out how fast Russell and Teddy will have to go if I'm going to get to Marnie's party. I'm just factoring in two kids versus one when a crumpled-up piece of paper falls in my lap. Immediately, I put my hand over it. Then, when I'm sure Mr. Courtney's not looking, I unwrap it. It says: *Going to Marine's lame party?*

I look around to see Declan staring down at me. He looks nervous; it's funny, that's just how I'd feel if I'd asked him if he was going.

Holding up the note, I nod. He smiles, gives a little thumbs-up.

That settles it. I am making it to Marnie's lame party—even if Russell and Teddy have to go at warp speed.

On Halloween night I have it all planned out. At 6:00 start getting dressed. By 6:15 put Mouli into his carrier, and by 6:30 start trick-or-treating. Be *done* trick-or-treating by 7:30 sharp. Then drop Teddy off at his dad's, jump into a cab, hurl Russell at our dad, and be at Marnie's party by 8:15. It's tricky, but I think I can do it. I told Declan I would be there, and I am going to be there.

Of course, Russell takes forever to put on his stupid costume, which is nothing more than a towel over his shoulders for a cape, a paper cone hat with some stars scribbled on it, and a chopstick for a wand. Mouli thrashes and howls as I push him inside his carrier. One of his claws catches my mom's shirt and puts a little rip in the sleeve. Well, that's what she gets for making me take Russell trick-or-treating.

By the time we leave, I'm already ten minutes behind schedule.

First we pick up Teddy Finster, Russell's best friend—an honor he got by being the only seven-year-old even dorkier than Russell. Teddy is dressed as Batman, which is odd because Teddy's not exactly Caped Crusader material. In fact, he's a horrendous wimp. Every time Mouli yowls, Teddy whimpers. Plus, he has a million and one food allergies, so every door we hit, he takes ages deciding if he can have this or that piece of candy. I tell myself that Mr. and Mrs. Finster have just separated, so I have to be nice to Teddy and not get annoyed by him.

We don't finish until 8:15. I promised Eve and Syd I'd be at the party by now. They're probably saying, *Where is that loser?* this very minute. As we head over to Teddy's dad's place, I tell myself that all I have to do is drop Teddy off, drop Russell off, and I am free. . . .

Thankfully, Teddy's dad lives only two blocks away. Mr. Finster's on the phone as he answers the door. He nods to us, then says into the cell, "Yeah, hold on a minute. Yeah, I just got to take my kid. . . ." He glances at us, then says irritably, "I'm gonna have to call you back."

I have a strange impulse to say, *Gee, don't bother just for us.* Instead, I say brightly, "Here's Teddy!"

I give Russell a tug as a signal that it's time for us to split. But Teddy's busy whispering something to him. Russell listens, then whispers something back.

Mr. Finster snaps his fingers at Teddy. "Come on, Teddy, let's go."

Russell gestures that he has something secret to tell me. I bend down, and he whispers in my ear, "Teddy wants to know if I can come trick-or-treating with him and his dad."

"No," I say shortly. "Dad's expecting us, and we've got to go."

Russell wails, "Ple-ease, Anna."

"Yeah, plee-eease, Anna," whines Teddy.

Mr. Finster presses for the elevator. "I'm not taking all night to do this, Teddy. Three seconds, and we're not going at all."

Teddy says, "Dad, can Russell come too?"

"Sure, I don't care." *Yeah, right,* I think, *because you can ignore two kids just as easily as one.*

Russell tugs on my tunic. "We can be a *little* late.

Come on, Anna, please, pleasepleaseplease? I got hardly *anything*. . . ."

"We can't be late for Dad," I say through clenched teeth. "He'll worry."

Teddy's dad holds up his cell. "What's his number? I'll leave a message."

For a second I think of giving him the wrong number. Then I look over at Russell and Teddy. From their puffed-out cheeks and wide-open eyes, I can tell they are holding their breath—they always do this because they think it brings them luck. I want to take Russell aside, explain to him that there's this party and that it's really important to me, that I will *buy* him the stupid candy. . . .

But it's not really about the candy; it's about Russell hanging with his friend. And Teddy not wanting to be left alone with his dad—and I can absolutely see why he wouldn't want that.

But I *have* to get to Marnie's party. I promised Declan I would be there. If I don't go, I am betraying the will of the cards.

Russell and Teddy run out of breath, gasp, then puff out their cheeks again.

I can't stand to see their faces if I say no.

Why can I never say no?

I give Mr. Finster my dad's number.

As expected, trick-or-treating with Teddy and his dad is a nightmare. Teddy's normal wimpishness turns into outright terror around his dad. When Mouli yowls and Teddy cringes, his dad sighs. "It's just a cat, it's not going to hurt you." When Teddy yells, "I'm Batman!" his dad tells him to keep it down, the whole world doesn't need to know. As we go down in the elevator, Russell takes hold of my hand, which he never does unless he's really nervous. After a moment Teddy takes the other one. I squeeze both to let them know it's okay, Mouli and I are here.

Because Teddy's so scared, he takes even longer to pick what candy he wants. This has his dad on the verge of exploding.

At the sixth door his dad suggests, "Why don't you take a lollipop?"

"I don't want a lollipop," says Teddy.

"Well, take something, pal. There's other kids waiting." Which is true. Behind us, a little girl in a bee costume looks seriously annoyed.

Teddy takes a mini Hershey's bar, then puts it back. Mr. Finster snatches it out of the bowl again, saying, "There are people waiting, so this is what you're having."

Teddy squeals, "No, I wanted the other one."

But his dad doesn't listen, just pulls him out of the line. I'm about to say, *Let him take what he wants,* when I hear, "That's o-okay, Mr. Finster. Ruby can wait."

The voice is deep, male, and sounds like a skipping CD. I look around to see where it came from—and find myself staring at Nelson Kobliner. He has bolts in his neck. His face is green. His head is rectangular, thanks to a rubber cap of black over his own dark hair. He is Frankenstein. And probably the only other kid in our grade not at Marnie's party.

Nelson/Frankenstein says to Teddy, "G-get what you . . . want." Teddy glances up at his dad, who looks like he's about to explode with impatience.

We all hold our breath as Teddy picks through the candy. Mr. Finster's fingers tighten.

Then Nelson says, "Y-you know, Mr. Finster?" There's a long pause; it seems like Nelson's forgotten what he meant to say. Then all at once he blurts out, "I can take Teddy. If you're busy."

At first I'm like, *Oh, great. Hey, Anna, you might not get to party with Declan, but you get to go trick-or-treating with Crazy Nelson Kobliner! Aren't you lucky?* I mean, the last time I saw this guy, I had just thrown a ball in his face.

Worst-case scenario: Nelson wants revenge for his humiliation. He will get it by mugging Russell for his Halloween loot.

Best-case scenario, which isn't all that hot either: Nelson doesn't want revenge, but the entire evening will be hideously awkward and embarrassing because Nelson is bizarre and I have nothing to say to him. Other than, *Gee, hope I didn't break your jaw.*

I look at Mr. Finster, praying he will rescue me and say no.

But, of course, given the chance to ditch his kid, he says brightly, "Great idea."

As our little group trucks down the stairs to the next floor, I look at my watch: 8:45. No way am I getting to Marnie's party now.

Nelson notices. "Kind of late, huh?"

Which feels like rubbing it in, so I stomp down the rest of the stairs, saying, "Yeah, just a little."

Then I remember Nelson's name crossed out, the jerk who wrote *Don't bother.* How can I feel sorry for myself for being late when he was purposely disinvited?

But I don't care. I'm fed up with being nice. Russell and Teddy are karate chopping a rubber garbage can; they don't care I'm missing the party. Mr. Finster doesn't care. My parents certainly don't. . . .

I put my thumb to the doorbell, press long and hard.

"Whoa," says Nelson. "I think they know we're here."

While the kids crowd around grabbing handfuls of junk, I lean against the wall, put my foot up on Mouli's carrier.

Nelson says, "Is that your cat?"

"My brother's familiar," I say sourly. "All great wizards have them."

"Oh, yeah," says Nelson. "If you don't mind my asking . . . what are . . . ?" He points vaguely to my costume.

"A fool," I tell him. "Come on, Russell."

Nelson is silent for the next two doors. But at the third one there's a bowl of mixed candy, so Teddy and Russell and even Ruby have a powwow on what Teddy should have. As we wait, I check my watch again: 9:05.

Then I hear Nelson say, "If you want to go, I can take the kids around. You know, maybe Russell can sleep over at Teddy's, or if you tell me where, I could drop him off. . . . I mean, if it's not . . . t-too far."

I have an image of Frankenstein Nelson showing up at my dad's with Russell in tow but no me. Minor flip-out on Dad's part to follow.

I look at Nelson. Obviously, I've made it pretty clear that hanging with him and a pack of kids is not my idea of a rocking Halloween. And still, Nelson was ready to do me this huge favor. Even though I smacked him in the face with a rubber ball. Even though I've been nothing but rude to him. Just so I can go to a party with people who wouldn't deign to be in the same room with him.

Uh, Mr. President, I'd like to nominate myself as Queen Jerk.

I say, "Nah, you don't have to do that. This is . . ."

Russell runs up and head butts me in the stomach. "Anna, I got your favorite! Mini Snickers! You can have it if you want." He presses it into my hand.

". . . this is cool."

As we move on to the next floor, I ask Nelson, "So, how do you know Teddy?"

"We live in the building." Nelson nods to Bee Girl. "That's my sister, Ruby."

"She's really cute."

"She's a . . . brat," Nelson says cheerfully. "On an atomic level. But she's okay—unless you mess with her Barbies." He hesitates. "Teddy's okay too. Better when his dad's not around."

Nelson has this funny, halting way of talking. It's one of the reasons people think he's retarded. But I wonder if he talks that way because he knows people think he's brain damaged and it makes him nervous.

Then Nelson asks, "How'd you get . . . ?"

It takes him so long to finish that I decide to guess. "Trick-or-treat duty?" He nods. "Mom's got class, Dad has to work. What about you?"

"My mom couldn't get home in time, so I don't mind."

The question's there, so I say carefully, "Your dad doesn't live around here?"

"We don't see him," says Nelson shortly. Then, before I can say I'm sorry or anything, he says, "Yeah, I . . . would have figured you'd be at the . . . you know."

Oh, God, does even Nelson know I have a crush on Declan? "How come?"

He gestures at my costume. "You look . . ."—his big green head bobbles—". . . like you were going to a . . . Something where you'd want to look . . . nice." He says the last word very quietly, almost not at all.

"Oh." I don't know what to say. Then the word comes, and I say it. "Thanks."

By 9:15 we've hit every single apartment in the building. Ruby is yawning and leaning against Nelson. I am carrying Russell's bag and Mouli. Only Teddy is still going, giving karate chops to everything in sight.

Nelson takes us down to the lobby before delivering Teddy back to his dad. I elbow Russell, who yawns out, "Thank you."

Nelson smiles. "You're welcome, man." He points to the carrier. "Cool familiar, by the way."

Then he looks at me. "Well . . ." Big wave of the hand.

"Yeah," I say, and give a big wave of the hand back.

When we get to my dad's, Russell plunges headlong onto the couch, pretending to faint from exhaustion. My dad smiles, says, "Big haul, huh?" Russell groans dramatically.

Then my dad says to me, "You have some messages. Eve called. Five times. Syd called twice." He hands me a slip of paper. "They implied I was keeping you locked in a closet somewhere." I take the piece of paper and go to the bedroom for privacy.

I try to decide whom to call first. As they're both at the party, I can't call one without the other knowing. I'd rather start with Syd, because she won't scream at me, but Eve will expect to be called first and will be mad if I don't. So I dial Eve. One ring and she picks up.

I say, "It's me."

"Where *are* you?" Eve hisses.

"We got . . . hung up."

Eve groans. It's weird. Going around with Nelson, I had almost forgotten the party. It was like it didn't matter. Now I feel it like a punch in the stomach. *I've missed it. I'm not there. Everyone's there but me. Declan is there . . . and Alexa is right there with him.*

I hear Syd saying, "Let me talk to her." Then, "Hey. What happened?"

"Fungus Toad had to hit a lot of apartments. We just got to my dad's now." I take a deep breath. "So, what's going on?"

"Uh . . ." My stomach drops. "Uh" is not what I wanted to hear. "Well, I really see why you think this guy is hot. He is way cute."

All of a sudden, I hear Eve again. "So, you're coming over now, right?"

I glance at myself in the mirror. The fabric on my hat has come loose and is dangling over my ear. I have mashed Snickers bar on my boots and a Life Saver stuck to my tights. Ruby put it there because she didn't like the green flavor. "I don't think so."

"What?" Eve wails. "No, Anna, you have to. Make your dad pay for a cab."

There's something in her voice that makes me ask, "Why? What's going on?"

"Nothing," says Syd sharply. Then I hear her whisper to Eve, "Forget it, it's not like it matters now anyway."

Suddenly, I feel wiped out with tiredness. I know I

should go, but I look rotten and I feel worse. I can't imagine showing up and having Declan say, *Oh, wow, you're amazing*. He's probably mad I didn't show. Probably figures, *Forget her. . . .*

I want to ask why it doesn't matter, why Syd's telling Eve to forget it. But there's no point. I know why. Fate told me to be at that party tonight, and I wasn't. And on Monday, I'll have to hear all about it, and when I do, I'll know it's my fault because I should have told my mom no and not been a wimp. I should have made Russell leave when we planned and not cared about bumming him out. But I didn't, and this is exactly what I get for being such a loser.

I hang up the phone before I start crying. Which, I guess, is a good thing.

SEVEN

THREE OF SWORDS

Strife, unhappiness, sorrow, opposition, disappointment

Yes, I swore to myself that I would not look at Zoe's World. But on Sunday night, I decide that if Alexa and Declan did hook up, I might as well be prepared. And, anyway, maybe Eve and Syd got it wrong. Maybe they misinterpreted what was going on.

But then Zoe's World comes up, and I know Eve and Syd weren't wrong at all.

Zoe's World, 11/1
A fab time was had by all at Marnie Stonor's sinister soiree. The usual suspects were present in most unusual costumes. First prize in bizarre went to Chico Goldfarb, who

came dressed as Polluted Carrot. Still trying to figure that one out, Chico!

Now on to the unmentionables—because that's what you really want to know, isn't it? Did GreekGod bestow his favors upon anyone? La Diva isn't talking, but maybe that's because she had something better to do with her tongue. . . .

As much as I knew something had happened, it twists my stomach to see the proof. I hate it, the very idea of Declan getting together with someone as cold as Alexa Roth. Okay, she's pretty, okay, she's in commercials, but she's so not a nice person. Why doesn't he see that? Why doesn't that matter?

Oh, right, Anna. He should only like qualities that you have. Like niceness and okay-lookingness. And boringness. Yeah, he should be really into boring—then you might have a shot.

I look at the cards sitting on my desk. The box is closed and quiet, like it's thinking something it doesn't want to say. But I can hear it anyway. *We had it all set up for you. You should have gone to that party, but you were scared. You didn't want to face Alexa and all the other P&Ps, in case you bombed out in front of your friends. That's why you said yes to your mom. That's why you didn't make*

Russell leave early. And that's why nothing interesting is ever going to happen to you, even when it's supposed to—because you didn't have any faith in us or yourself.

Monday morning, Eve says, "Are we ready for this?"

I say, "We are ready."

And we go into school, braced for the sight of the new supercouple.

As we trudge up the stairs, Eve says, "Allow me to say that this sucks. Big-time. It's a victory for everything bogus in this world. Declan is a former freak," she says heatedly. "He's got no business with some Little Miss Perfect. And you *know* Alexa won't let anyone forget for a second that she has him. She'll be hanging off him, going, 'Look, everybody, see what I got.' And we're all supposed to go, 'Ooh, how wonderful, they're in love.'" She swings her book bag against the wall in frustration. "Uck. The whole thing is toxic."

I sigh. "The only thing we can do is ignore it."

Eve's not the only one who's down. Any girl who's ever been snubbed by an über-cool or insulted by a P&P is quiet today. Finally, we had one of our own who was a hottie—and what does he do? Ditch us for Alexa Roth.

Of course, the P&Ps can't stop talking about it. Everywhere I go, I hear, "Were you at the party when it happened?" "I was so there." "Oh, my God, what actually happened?"

And, of course, Alexa doesn't miss a single opportunity to let everyone know she and Declan are together. At lunch she makes a grand entrance, pulling Declan along like he's some dumb toy.

It feels better to tell myself that I never really had a shot with Declan, that I got silly over some stupid cards a crazy old lady left me. Then I can see it the way Eve does: an annoying victory for the über-cools. It's only when I remember how Declan's face lit up when I apologized for the tipped tray that I feel like I lost something.

I don't get it. How could he even think of liking me, then switch over to someone so different? And so fast? Is that what guys are like?

"We are so ditching Turkey Trot," says Eve as she watches Alexa nibble on Declan's ear. "Can you imagine how obnoxious they'll be at an official school thing? Nightmare."

Oh, God, the Turkey Trot, our "big dance" at Harvest Festival. I had forgotten all about that. Eve's right, no way are we going. It's hard enough to see Declan sitting next to Alexa in Subzero. Seeing them at a dance . . .

I put my sandwich down. My stomach's too tight to eat.

As much I used to look forward to chorus because I could see Declan, now I dread it for the same reason. I refuse to even look at him. At one point Bridget whispers, "I think someone is trying to get your attention," and points in Declan's direction. I shrug, look the other way.

I am determined not to like Declan anymore.

At the end of class Mr. Courtney shouts, "Hey, Anna! I need to talk to you."

I approach the piano, wondering if he's going to yell at me for being in a bad mood.

Mr. Courtney says, "Here's my problem. Every year you all put on a Thanksgiving pageant for the first and second graders?" I nod, remembering how I used to sit on the gym floor while some kid dressed up as a turkey ran around trying to get away from the mean farmer who was trying to kill him. Even then, I thought it was creepy.

Mr. Courtney continues. "Last year Ms. Kenworthy asked me to take over the pageant. I did, and it was a great success—primarily because I played the farmer. You know the deal: I wander around with an ax, going, 'Where's Tom Turkey? I want Tom Turkey . . .' Blah, blah, blah."

He fixes his eye on me. "I need a Tom Turkey. Or Tammy Turkey, if you prefer."

I gulp. "I thought Megan Schultz was the turkey."

"Yeah, Megan's flaked out on me this year."

That's right. After last year Megan swore she'd never do it again. I can't remember exactly what she said, but basically it was ax + Mr. Courtney = bad things.

"So what do you say? This is a starring role. Scarlett O'Turkey Burger . . ."

Just what I need: death by dismemberment. Can I say I'll be sick? That my family celebrates some strange holiday instead of Thanksgiving and we'll be away? That religious principles forbid me from dressing up as an animal?

"Don't worry," says Mr. Courtney crossly. "I'll make sure you have plenty of time to make it to the dance."

"No, that's not it, it's . . ."

"It's what?"

"It's . . . it's . . ." I can't think of what it is! God, why am I such a wimp?

I swallow, say, "It's . . . great."

The following week Ms. Buffala, the art teacher, asks if I could possibly help her decorate the gym for the Turkey Trot. Even though I'm not going to the dance, I say yes, because Ms. Buffala cries if people are mean to her.

The day after that, Ms. Kenworthy asks if I think we'll beat last year's record for donated canned goods. I go, "Yeah, hope so!" Because what do you say? *My life is a misery right now, and I don't care about poor people going hungry.*

So now I have to make sure I bring a lot of cans to the Harvest Festival.

Decorating gyms for dances you're not going to go to. Schlepping canned goods. Playing a turkey. This is my life. The life of a wimp.

Actually, as humiliating as it will be to play Tammy Turkey, the rehearsals do keep my mind off of Declan and Alexa—who people now call "DNA." For "D&A." (Say it fast, you'll get it.) Worrying that someone might hack you to death with an ax puts things into perspective. Not that I think Mr. Courtney wants to kill me. Just that if his rehearsals with the hockey stick are anything to go by, he makes a very convincing homicidal maniac.

I try to keep out of DNA's way. But it's hard, because even if I don't see Declan and Alexa, I'm always hearing about them. Everywhere you go, there are "I heards": "I heard he's been crazy about her for months." "I heard they were passing notes in assembly." "I heard they went to the movies and almost got thrown out, they were making out so much." "I heard she says she'll lose her mind if he ever dumps her."

I don't even look at Zoe's World anymore because it's turned into a DNA blog. Any second, Declan and Alexa will have their own reality series.

I did see them once. They were hanging out on the front steps with some of Alexa's buds. Alexa was chattering away to her friends. Declan was just sitting there, playing with his shoelace. As I passed by, Declan looked up, called out, "Hey . . ." I stopped, just in time to see Alexa nudge his arm and say, "Hey, Dec. What was that show you were telling me about?"

I knew to keep walking.

One day at lunch Eve says, "Did you see Zoe's World yesterday?" I shake my head. "I think you might want to look at it."

"Why?"

"She pointed out that Declan looks embarrassed every time Alexa plays with his hair in that way she thinks is oh-so-cute."

"Really?" For a second I feel a weird surge of hope. Then I think, *So what? So Declan doesn't like it when Alexa plays with his hair. It's got nothing to do with me.*

Eve says casually, "Maybe we should go to Turkey Trot."

"I thought we were ditching."

"Yeah, but now I think it might be worth going to."

I consider. If DNA is a fact of life, I might as well get used to it. And why should I let Alexa stop me from going to the dance? Who knows? Maybe there'll be someone there I was destined—ha-ha—to be with.

"Okay. On one condition: You stay by me the whole time"—Eve nods—"and you help me get out of my turkey costume. Because if anybody over seven sees me in it, I'll die."

"Deal," says Eve.

Anna's To-Do List for Harvest Festival
Wednesday, November 25

9:00: Deliver cans to school for canned food drive. (Use double bag!)

12:00: Help Ms. Buffala hang orange and brown crepe paper in the gym.

1:30: Put on turkey costume in second-floor bathroom. Make Eve act as guard.

2:00: Do Thanksgiving pageant with Mr. Courtney. Survive.

3:00: Find Eve. Take off turkey costume. Pray no one has seen me.

3:30: Go to Turkey Trot. Ignore DNA!

At 8:15 the morning of the Turkey Trot, I check the bag of canned goods I put by the door last night and remove four ancient cans of cranberry sauce. Every year my mom tries to sneak in nasty stuff she bought on sale a hundred years ago and never used. Why she thinks poor people want old cranberry sauce any more than we do, I don't know.

I lift the cans off the floor to test the strength of the double bag. It's heavy, but it should hold, particularly with four fewer cans.

When I'm ready to leave for school, Russell is waiting for me by the door. Today he has two straws stuck behind his ears.

I say, "I give up."

"I'm a bull," he says, and snorts his way out the door. I hoist the bag up. The handle gives just a little, but if I walk very, very slowly, I think it'll be okay.

The handle gives out by the second block. So now I have to carry the stupid bag in my arms. It is really, really heavy. By the third block I am panting. My heart is pounding. I may have a stroke. I set the bag down on the ground, say to Russell, "One-minute break."

He whines, "I don't want to miss the chocolate turkeys." The school gives out chocolate turkeys to the little kids, because, you know, they need to be *more* hyper. But it's a big thing to Russell, so I take a deep breath and lift the bag up again.

Immediately, there is a horrible ripping sound. Then a clang as the first can hits the pavement.

"Why are you carrying creamed corn?" asks Eve as I trundle up the steps to school. I tell her it's a very long story.

"Hey," she says as I dump the cans into the food bin. "Guess who was *not* seen having lunch with a certain someone yesterday?"

"Guess who doesn't care?"

"I think there's definitely trouble in paradise."

Wouldn't you know it? At the very mention of the word "trouble"—or maybe it was "paradise"— Alexa and Declan come through the door. Actually, Alexa comes in, then waits for Declan to catch up with her. A second later he shuffles in, his hands stuffed in the pockets of his army jacket, head down, his hair all in his face. He almost walks past Alexa, but she grabs him by the arm and says, "Right here, silly." Then she plants a big kiss on his cheek.

I think: *PDA, very tacky. Not Declan's style at all.*

Apparently, Declan agrees, because he jerks away from her and heads toward the stairs.

Eve gives a low whistle. You never, but never, see Alexa Roth get burned like that.

Alexa hears it and flushes a deep, ugly red. She glares at us, then follows Declan up the stairs.

12:00: Help Ms. Buffala hang orange and brown crepe paper in the gym.

Ms. Buffala is deep into the environment, and she's a very wonderful human being—but sometimes she goes too far. Recycling last year's crepe paper? Too far.

Standing on a ladder, I tape a long droopy strand to the basketball hoop, then look down at Ms. Buffala and call, "What do you think?" She gives a thumbs-up.

Then she says, "I brought some gourds for decoration. They're in the supply room."

Wanting to get away from limp crepe paper, I say, "I'll get them." I take the keys from Ms. Buffala and go across the gym to the supply room.

As I open the supply room door, I regret my offer. The place is creepy, crowded with all sorts of junk. Anyone could be lurking in here.

Mrs. Buffala said the gourds were in a shopping bag on the floor, so I keep my eyes trained downward. I see a concrete floor, a mop and bucket, some old textbooks . . .

A pair of sneakers. With feet in them.

They're sticking out from under a metal shelf, but they disappear the second I walk by. Whomever they're attached to is hiding behind the shelf. For a moment I think: *Leave them alone.* Then, curious, I set aside cans of paint and reams of paper and peer through the shelf to see . . . Nelson Kobliner.

I whisper, "Hey. What're you doing here?"

"Hiding," he says. "You?"

"Decorating. For the 'big dance.' Yay."

He nods. "Reasons number one through five hundred twenty-three that I'm hiding. I don't g-get those things. Kind of . . . torture, I don't know."

"I know. You're right." It feels really weird to be talking to Nelson like he's anyone else. It helps that he's sitting down, not towering over me. "How's Ruby?"

"Good. Ballet's, like, her big thing now."

"Hey, a bee ballet." He smiles, and I notice his notebook, the one he's always carrying around. "Can I ask, what is that?"

"Uh . . ." He ducks his head. "Something I'm working on."

"Oh, yeah?"

"Yeah . . ." His head sways from side to side. "Ack, awkward alert."

"Why?"

"You'll think it's stupid."

"Won't, I swear."

He stares at the notebook like he's asking its permission. "It's a . . . you know, graphic novel thingy. I call it *The Greatest Graphic Novel Ever,* but that's . . . strictly a joke."

Nelson writing a novel. And illustrating a novel. I can't believe it. The book is thick, the edges of the pages are speckled with ink. He's obviously done a ton of work on it. "What's it about?"

He frowns, picks at the edges. "Oh, doom, treachery, end-of-the-world kind of stuff."

"Wow." I wonder if that's how school feels to him. Wouldn't blame him if it did. Actually, these days, that's what it feels like to me, too.

I say, "Well, you should come to the dance. Lots of doom and treachery there. Be good for your book."

Nelson half smiles. "Uh, no. Rather be . . . flayed alive with a rusty chain saw."

"Gotcha. Well, if it gets too bad, maybe I'll sneak back here." Nelson looks up. For a moment I wonder if he thinks I'm teasing him. "I mean, if you don't mind intruders." I say "intruders" like Ark-Ark does, *"Intruders, intruders."*

"You don't . . ." Nelson glances down at his book. "You don't look like an intruder."

Which I don't get, but it makes me laugh anyway. As I leave, I keep the door open just a crack. I don't want anyone to lock Nelson in. It's nice to think of him lurking in there while all the Harvest Festival madness goes on.

1:30: Put on turkey costume in second-floor bathroom. Make Eve act as guard.

Since the show is for the first and second graders, Eve and I meet in the kiddie bathroom on the second floor. The sinks are lower, the toilets are dinkier; it makes you feel like a giant in midgetland.

Lifting up the bag with the costume in it, Eve says, "I could tell Courtney you're sick."

"Let's just get it over with," I say. Eve pulls a pair of rubber turkey feet out of the bag. These go over my socks. Then there's a feathered, padded stomach that goes over my shirt. Next are the wings, two big ovals, painted in red and brown patches for feathers. You have to strap them on to your arms, which is why I need Eve's help. Once they're on, your hands are useless.

I give a practice flap. "How do I look?"

"A vision. Ready for the final humiliation?"

"I'm ready."

She reaches up and slides two pieces of elastic over my head, fixing them behind my ears. I look in the mirror to find I now have a beak and a long, red, rubber turkey wattle dangling from my chin. I shake my head a little, watch the wattle swing.

Eve says, "You know Megan Schultz needed stitches last year—you know that, right? Manic Music Man almost chopped her legs off."

My stomach turns over, but I say, "He did not. Megan tripped, then told everyone Mr. Courtney tried to kill her so she wouldn't seem like a klutz."

"Uh-*huh*," says Eve, like she knows the real deal. "Well, it's been nice knowing you."

"Thanks." I check that my feathers are in place. "Meet me back here at three o'clock, right? I got to get out of this thing before the dance." Eve smiles evilly. "I mean it, Eve, three o'clock. I'm not kidding."

"Okay, okay . . ."

2:00: Do Thanksgiving pageant with Mr. Courtney. Survive.

A few minutes later I'm standing outside the door to the assembly hall. Inside are hundreds of little kids, sitting in near darkness. Russell is in there somewhere; I have bribed him with extra Mouli days not to tell anyone that Tammy Turkey and I are one and the same.

Mr. Courtney said the teachers would leave the aisles free for me to run up and down, but I know I'm going to step on some kid and squash him. Or hit him in the face with my wing.

Luckily, all the doors in the school open when you push this bar in the middle of them, so even though I can't use my hands, I can still open the door.

Okay, take a deep breath. . . .

Throw self against door. . . .

Burst in screaming, "Oh, kids, help me, help me! It's Thanksgiving, and the evil, cruel Farmer Brown is after me! I don't want to lose my head!"

I run up and down the aisles, imploring kids to hide me. As rehearsed, I make some kids stand in front of me to hide me, while the rest yell, "We still see you!" I kneel down, flapping anxiously, and they cry, "Still see you!" As I run to hide behind the window blinds, I hear Russell tell the kid next to him, "That's my sister." So much for bribery.

Then I hear the assembly hall door crash open. Mr. Courtney bellows, "Where is Tammy Turkey? . . . I want Tammy Turkey!"

He stalks into the hall. He is carrying a very large ax.

The kids shriek, *"Run!"*

So I do. Three times around the hall, then up and down the aisles, while Mr. Courtney chases me, roaring, "Come here, you turkey! It's cookin' time!"

I'm almost out of breath by the time I have to collapse on the floor and cry, "Please, kids—you don't really want to eat me, do you?" (Really, the whole thing is very warped.)

They all yell, *"Nooooo!"*

Mr. Courtney swings around. "What? You don't want savory, juicy turkey on Thanksgiving Day?"

Another cry of *"Nooooo!"*

"You'd rather have yucky brown rice and yogurt and that disgusting green Jell-O with the weird bits in it?"

The kids aren't so sure, and I yell, "How about chocolate ice cream?"

They cheer. Tammy is saved.

As we bow, Mr. Courtney says, "You were magnificent. Gave me a lot of ideas for next year."

Before I can say I intend to study in Timbuktu next year and will not be available, Russell races up and throws his arms around me. "You were awesome. Can I wear your feet?"

Over his head, I see the clock: 3:00.

> 3:00: Find Eve. Take <u>off</u> turkey costume. Pray no
> one has seen me.

Only . . . one question.

WHERE IS EVE??

It is 3:15. I have been flapping in the bathroom for a quarter of an hour now. I am still a turkey! Forget Farmer Brown—if anyone sees me, I'll drop dead of embarrassment.

Of course, no one is around to witness my shame because they're all at the STUPID DANCE! Probably with Eve! Who has obviously forgotten me entirely. I will kill her when I see her, I will *kill* her.

By knocking my beak against a stall door, I manage to get that off my face. Next, I try to get the wattle off. But when I reach up, all I do is poke myself in the eye with a cardboard feather. I have to calm down. I have to get help.

I push open the door to the bathroom a crack, say, "Hello? Anybody out there?"

No one answers. Of course. All the lower-school people are long gone. The only people left in the building are at the dance. Three floors above me.

Can I possibly, possibly walk home dressed as a turkey? No.

Would Eve do this on purpose? I can't believe that. She might joke, but she would never actually . . .

Maybe she's trying to get downstairs to me. Maybe she ran into someone. Or maybe . . . does she think we said meet *at* the dance? She can't think that. But maybe she thinks we said meet on the stairwell? Maybe she's waiting for me there and wondering where I am.

I have to get up there. Before she goes back inside to the dance.

Very carefully, I push open the bathroom door and step outside. Then, as quietly as possible, I tiptoe to the door leading to the stairwell and push it open. As I do, I pray no one has come down here to make out.

I'm in luck. They haven't. For a moment I wait, listening for anyone who might be on the upper floors. But all I hear is the *thump, thump* of the music in the gym. I start climbing and immediately rediscover that it is very hard to walk up stairs frontward with rubber feet. So I must walk backward, thereby improving on my earlier dorkiness.

Finally, I get to the top floor. No Eve. So much for my theory. The door to the gym has a glass square in it so you can see in. I peek in and see Eve talking to Paul Harvie. Obviously, she was headed downstairs to meet me when she ran into him near the door. Paul is cute—but not so cute that I will forgive Eve for not coming to help me. No one on earth is that cute.

I rap on the window with my wing, hoping she'll hear me. She doesn't. The music is too loud. Or Paul is too cute or whatever. I rap a little harder. I can't knock too loud because I don't want anyone but Eve looking to see who's knocking.

Oh, God, Eve is walking away! She's headed toward the art room. I have to get her attention before she disappears! So I push the door open the tiniest crack, thinking I will hiss, *Psst! Eve!* But it's hard to know how much you're pushing when you're inside a padded costume. And I guess I push too hard, because all of a sudden, I'm stumbling into the gym.

And everyone—I mean, *everyone*—is staring.

And then they crack up laughing.

It's like some horrible nightmare, the one where you're walking to school and you're naked. Except in this one I'm wearing a turkey outfit, and it is much, much worse. I turn around to flee and find Marnie blocking the door. I raise a wing to swat her and feel someone grab me by the tail feathers. I hear, "Well, gobble, gobble."

Alexa.

Marnie laughs. "Yeah—gobble, gobble, gobble."

I say, "Okay, whatever . . ." Like, *Ha-ha, hilarious, now let me go.* But Alexa slips her arm around my shoulders, guides me away from the door.

"Where are you going? It's Thanksgiving." Then she yells to the crowd gathering around us: "You have to have turkey on Thanksgiving, right?" There's some "Yeahs" and more laughter. Just a joke, right? Only I can see Alexa's eyes, and I know it's not a joke.

"Hey, let's see a turkey trot," shouts Alexa, shoving me into the middle of the dance floor. "Yeah, trot!" someone yells. It's all gotten so nasty so fast, I don't know what to do. Right now the only thing I feel capable of is crying—and that's the last thing I want.

I hear Eve shout, "Leave her alone, you jerks!" But she's drowned out by everyone yelling, "Trot, trot, trot . . ." It's a chant now.

I keep thinking, *This is dumb, it's not happening.* Or that any second, it'll stop and people will go back to normal. Only I may fall apart before that happens.

Frantic, I look for someone I know, a friendly face. I see Bridget, way in the back by the doors. She's wide-eyed, watching, like she hates what's going on but doesn't know what to do. Kelly Greenspan from

French, also just staring. Nicky Froehlich . . . all these people who are usually my friends, and not one of them will say, *Stop it. Cut it out.*

Because no one wants to be a freak, the one everyone yells at and laughs at. And when you are the freak, no one will take your side.

The door to the supply room opens, and Nelson comes out. I guess he heard all the screaming and came out to see what was going on. Seeing him, I get it. This is what it feels like to be him every day.

Then I feel someone approach. At this point any help is humiliating, so I let fly with my wing.

Then I hear, "Hey, whoa."

Declan. If he says one stupid thing, I will punch him out. I don't care how gorgeous he is.

He says, "You want to dance?"

Of course. Dance, trot, very funny. Taking Alexa's stupid joke one step further. I want to say, *You know, it's really sad when people date jerks and turn into jerks themselves. Or maybe you always were a jerk.* But I don't trust my voice.

Instead, I get out a "Ha-ha."

"No, really."

"Yeah, I bet. Forget it."

Gently, he reaches under the wings and takes my hands. Then he takes a little dance step to the left. I follow, worried the costume will rip if I don't. Mr. Courtney would never forgive me.

Declan moves to the right. So do I. Somehow we're dancing.

But there is no laughter. No more yelling "Trot!"

"So how come you weren't at Marnie's lame party?" he asks.

It's pointless to lie. When you're dressed as a turkey, any pretension to be cool is blown.

"I had to take my little brother trick-or-treating."

"Oh." He nods. "Were you wearing . . . ?" He waves his hand at my turkey stomach.

"No, I was wearing something . . ."—*something that I wanted you to see me in, but you didn't, and even if you had, you wouldn't have cared because of Ms. Alexa*—". . . really nice."

Then someone puts on a slow song. I go red, worried that Declan will think I planned this somehow. I try to step back, let him know it's okay if he wants to stop now. But he slides his arm around my costume as if dancing with a turkey is no strange thing. I feel him patting around my costume, trying to figure out where to put his hands.

He says, "Well, I was bummed you weren't there."

"Yeah, I heard," I say sarcastically.

Now it's Declan's turn to go red.

I feel the entire room staring, but I don't look. Not for Eve, not even for Alexa. I don't care who's watching. I don't care about anything but Declan. I so want to look at him, but I'm scared I'll be all goofy and worshipping and embarrass him.

To his shoulder, I say, "This was seriously nice of you, thanks."

"It's not *nice*, it's . . ."

He hesitates, and I look up. As I do, Declan looks down.

And that's when he kisses me.

EIGHT

THE PAGE OF SWORDS, UPSIDE DOWN

*Imposter, powerlessness in the face
of stronger forces, unprepared*

Zoe's World, 11/26
GreekGod Has Chosen!!!

GreekGod made his official choice at last Wednesday's Turkey Trot—and Dumped Diva was there to witness all! (We're talking big-time dis, people, major ouch.)

So who's the lucky girl who pulled the victory out from under Dumped Diva's oh-so-perfect (but not surgically enhanced, oh, never!) nose? Well, she may have been a ChorusGrl, but she's definitely a star now.

✳

On Thanksgiving Day, Russell screams and runs out of the room when my mother sets the turkey down on the table. She finds him on his bed, sobbing, "You killed Tammy. You killed Tammy. . . ." He's so hysterical, Mom has to order Chinese for him.

While Mom calls, I sit at the table, thinking how strange it is that my entire life has changed and no one in my family has the slightest clue. I feel like a totally different person—but all they see is the same old Anna who waits patiently while Russell throws a fit and Mom deals and doesn't mind that dinner's getting cold.

Actually, New Anna is happy to wait, because I honestly couldn't care less about turkey or Chinese food or even Thanksgiving. Being alone just gives me more time to think about Declan.

I am now Declan's girlfriend.

Girlfriend of Declan.

G.O.D.

I know I shouldn't be thinking this way. You probably get in trouble for comparing yourself to a god just because a guy likes you. But I can't help thinking there's something a little divine about Declan. Okay, a lot divine. And in ancient times, when mortals were loved by gods, didn't they become sort of godlike too?

I can't believe I ever mistrusted the cards. All the

misery they predicted did come true, what with missing Marnie's party and having to deal with DNA. But after that—voilà! The Lovers! Happiness! G.O.D.!

The buzzer rings. Russell's moo goo gai pan is here.

First thing next morning, Syd, Eve, and I meet up at Café 96 for breakfast. "Okay," says Syd as we sit down. "Tell me *everything*. Do not leave out a single detail."

Eve leans forward. "It was amazing. A complete and total victory."

Syd bops her on the head with her spoon. "Let Anna tell it."

Syd looks at me, and I say, "It was actually pretty amazing. Uh . . ." For a second I'm stymied. I mean, you don't want to go on and on: *Let me tell you how incredible I am.*

Without thinking, I glance over at Eve, who says promptly, "Alexa was being Cow of the Universe, and Declan stepped in and said, 'No way, you and I are through. I am with Anna now.'"

Syd's eyes widen. "He *said* that?"

I shake my head. "Not exactly."

"He might as well have," says Eve. "He basically gave the finger to every über-cool there."

Syd gives her an exasperated look, then turns to me. "Just start at the beginning."

And I do, telling Syd the whole story, from when I put on the turkey feet to the moment Alexa stormed out of the gym in tears. As I describe it, I watch her and Eve's faces. They are paying complete attention to every word I'm saying. Not just because they're my friends and they love me, but because they're really, really interested. It's like I'm a movie and they're hooked. It makes sense; if this had happened to one of them, I'd be the same way.

Congratulations, Anna! You're interesting for a change.

Then Eve asks, "What'd he say when Alexa ran out?"

I try to remember. "I don't think he noticed."

Syd's eyes narrow; she thinks that's a little cold. I say quickly, "I think his back was to her. I don't think he saw."

Eve says, "If you knew this chick, you so wouldn't care, believe me."

"No, just . . ." Syd shrugs. "It doesn't matter." She grins at me. "Wild how the cards were so right."

Eve nods. "That they were."

Yeah, I think. *They were. Thanks, Mrs. Rosemont.*

"It's going to be crazy on Monday," says Eve. "I can't wait to see how the P&Ps deal. They are going to freak en masse."

Syd gives her a strange look. "Who cares if they freak? Who cares what they think, period?"

"Sydney," says Eve patiently, "you don't go to our school. You have no idea what a serious deal this is. I mean, they had this list of girls who were supposed to go out with Declan? And they're all gorgeous and tall and . . . total snot cows, right? And Declan could have asked any of them out. But he picked Anna instead."

She grins at me. But for some reason, what Eve just said doesn't make me feel great. *They were all gorgeous and tall . . . Declan could have asked any of them out. But he picked Anna instead.*

Why *did* Declan pick me?

Syd says, "Well, not to change the subject from the epic battle between good and evil, but I was thinking maybe soon we could try calling Tatiana's new owner. See how it's going, you know?"

Immediately, I say, "Yeah, we should definitely do that." Because as I much as I love being the one who's got something exciting going on, I want to show that I'm not going to be one of those obnoxious people who are like, *Oh, you're just my friend friends, fine for when* he's *not around, but when he is, who cares about you?*

I hate people like that.

As we leave the restaurant, Eve asks, "So, have you guys talked? Has he called?"

"No," I say, feeling some of my happiness leak away. "But it was Thanksgiving, right?"

"Right," says Syd. "You don't call on holidays."

That night my mom makes turkey sandwiches with lots of mayo on white toast. This, to me, is the best way to eat turkey. I wish we could skip the whole bird and get straight to the sandwiches. Russell has the rest of his moo goo gai pan.

As we eat, I listen for the phone. But it doesn't ring. I guess you don't call the day after holidays, either.

Back in my room I check to see if Zoe has posted anything new. It's the third time I've checked today. I really should stop. But I can't help it. I keep hoping to see something like, *GreekGod confesses he has always loved ChorusGrl. Diva just an unfortunate mistake.*

Nothing new.

I do kind of wish he'd call. Not that I'm worried or anything. But tomorrow we're going to my dad's, and if Declan calls then, I won't be here.

When the phone rings, I figure it's my dad calling to make arrangements. My mom yells, "Anna, for you," and I pick up, say, "Hey, D—"

Declan says, "Hey."

I am so stunned with relief that I am incapable of speech.

"Hello, you there?"

"Yes! Absolutely. Hi." My mind is blank. "Wow. So . . ."

"For a turkey, you kiss pretty good."

I feel myself go violently red. "Uh, so do you, for a nonturkey." He laughs. "So . . ."

"So."

I want to ask about Alexa, if she's upset about what happened or if she's giving him a hard time. But that seems private, like it's none of my business.

Then Declan says, "I want to ask you something, but I don't know if it's cool or not."

I hesitate, then say, "Sure, go ahead."

He takes a deep breath. "The thing is, I don't want to get all crazy."

I say, "Right," even though I'm not sure what "all crazy" means.

"I don't want to do the whole 'Oh, they're going out, look, there they are eating lunch' thing, you know?"

I think of Alexa in the school lobby forcing that kiss on him. "Yeah, I get that."

"Yeah?" He sounds relieved.

"Uh, sure." I have to fight not to say, *But does that mean we're not going out? Is this your way of taking it all back? Am I not, in fact, G.O.D.?*

Then he says, "I mean, I don't want . . ." He pauses. "I'm messing this up."

I take a breath, then say quickly, "You want to hang out, but you don't want the whole world knowing about it." I cross my fingers that he will say yes, that he will not say, *No, actually, I don't want to hang with you, period.*

But he says, "Yeah. That . . . that sounds cool." Then, "So, see you in chorus?"

"Yeah. I won't be in feathers, though. I hope that's okay."

He laughs. "I'll survive."

As I hang up, I wonder if I should have said what I did about hanging but not letting the whole world know. If I should have waited for Declan to finish saying what it was he didn't want. I feel like I can hear his voice in my head. And what it's saying is very different.

I don't want to go out with you.

I don't want to go out with anyone.

I go to my desk, look at the notebook where Syd wrote down the reading. There it is at the end: the Lovers card.

So I shouldn't worry.

On Monday morning I choose my outfit with care. This is my first day at school as G.O.D., and I want to look good. On the other hand, I don't want to overdo it. I've decided: Declan is absolutely right. I do not want to be one of those annoying "Oh, look at us" couples.

So when Eve asks if Declan called, I say, "Yeah" and that's *it*.

Only maybe I don't want to talk about Declan— but everyone else at school does. I'm barely done putting stuff in my locker when Amy Dermot, who I know from French, runs up to me and says, "You so have to tell me what happened at the dance!" All of a sudden, a lot of people who have never said hello to me before are going, "Hey, Anna," "Hi, Anna," "How's it going?" I even get a few friendly "Gobble, gobbles."

Any girl who's ever been dissed by the P&Ps is suddenly my best friend. In algebra Stacey Kantor whispers, "Just give me a number, one to ten."

"One to ten what?"

"*Declan.*"

In French, Kylie Chenoweth gives me the thumbs-up sign, then the "Call me" sign. In English, Sara Reynolds passes me a note: *Lunch?* Dara Williams stops in the hallway to say, "You don't know how glad I am that you stopped that whole DNA mess."

But it's not just the Freak Patrol. When Eve and I go to lunch, everyone looks up as we enter the cafeteria. It takes me a second to figure it out.

They want to see if I'm with Declan.

Uh, no, sorry, just Eve.

Still, lots of people say hi to me as we make our way to the table—even some people who were yelling "Trot!" at the dance. As I smile to someone I don't even know, I think, *This is what it's like to be a P&P. This is why they're so thin; they probably never make it to their table to eat lunch.*

Eve stalks ahead and gets us a table.

But as we sit down to eat, Elissa Maxwell glides by on her way to the Subzero Zone. Stopping, she says, "Hey, there" in a really friendly voice. Like she's not Elissa Maxwell and I'm not Turkey Girl. Like we're both . . . normal, the same.

Then she says, "You eating with anybody?"

Slightly embarrassing, because Eve is sitting right there.

Eve snaps, "No, she's not sitting with *anyone.*"

Elissa gives one of her smiles—the one that says, *I can smile at you no matter how rude you are because you're nothing and I'm a goddess*—then whispers to me, "Another time, okay? Like your skirt."

This is when I realize that I am the worst person in the world because despite the fact that she has just mortally insulted my best friend, I am the tiniest bit thrilled that Elissa Maxwell approves of my clothes and wants to have lunch with me.

When Elissa's gone, I say to Eve, "Well, that was a little crazy."

"*Yeah.*" Eve rips open a bag of chips and empties it onto her plate. Then she says, "I mean, trying to get with Declan through you? Pretty crass."

I nod. Although, actually, I did not know that Elissa was trying to get with Declan through me. I just thought she wanted to have lunch. But Eve is probably right. She usually is about these things.

Then Eve says, "Hey, by the way? I seriously need your help with algebra. I tried doing this assignment over the weekend, and it was just like, no way."

I nod. "Cool. After school we can do it during *Dumb, Rich, and Famous.*"

Eve glances around the cafeteria. "Interesting that Ms. Diva didn't show. Guess she couldn't take the humiliation." Ultracasual, she asks, "Have you seen her yet?"

I shake my head.

"I bet she and Declan had some mega blowup." She looks up from her chips.

"I don't know."

Eve peers at me. She wants blood and gore, but I

don't want to talk about Alexa. In fact, I'd like to forget Declan ever went out with her.

Finally, Eve sits back, says, "Yeah, who wants details?"

After that, we don't say much. Eve finishes her chips, says, "Ready?" and I nod.

But as we start to leave, I see Alexa come in.

Even worse, she sees me.

We're right in each other's path. I can go only one way: toward the door. Alexa, on the other hand, could go stand on line, head to someone's table. I really, really hope she does one of those things.

It's best not to say anything to her or even look at her. Whatever I do is going to feel like gloating: *Nyah, nyah, I've got him, you don't.*

I put my head down, keep walking.

I think: If she says something, just say you don't want to get into it.

Oh, God, she's coming my way.

I hear Eve whisper, "Just be cool. She cannot hurt you."

I think: *And maybe she doesn't want to. Maybe she's just headed to Subzero. She probably doesn't want anything more to do with me than I want to do with her.*

I'm still not looking, so when the shove comes, I am totally not prepared. It knocks my bag right off my shoulder, knocks me off balance; I step back and almost land in the garbage can.

I'm not quite sure how to breathe.

My shoulder actually hurts.

Eve is kneeling down, patting me. "Are you okay?"

You know how it is when someone says that? You suddenly realize, *Whoa, if someone has to ask me if I'm okay, I must not be okay.*

For a weird second I feel like I'm going to cry. I don't even know why. So, Alexa walked into me. Big deal.

She didn't just walk into you. She shoved you. Like, Get out of my way.

But it wasn't even really the shove. It was the feeling behind the shove. It was: *I hate you.*

Eve turns. "No way does she get away with this."

Frantic, I pull her back. "No, just . . . leave it. It didn't happen. It doesn't matter." I don't know why, but I'm totally panicked at the idea of a fight. All I want is to be out of here.

Which Eve must see, because she says, "Okay. Whatever you say." She pats my arm. "No bloodshed, I promise."

And we leave the cafeteria.

My stomach is in knots for the rest of the day. Everywhere I go, I am terrified I'll run into Alexa again. I've never had anyone hate me before. I have no idea how to handle it. I feel weak, stupid . . .

Unprepared. The cards predicted this. They said I would be powerless, unprepared to deal with threat. Is this what they meant? If so, how long does it go on? I thought all the competition and weirdness would be over once the Lovers came to be.

I keep wondering what else Alexa might do. Bad-mouth me all over school? What can she say? It wasn't like I tried to take Declan away from her. It just sort of . . . happened.

In the bathroom Kelly Dunphy comes up to me and says, "Are you okay? I heard what happened. God, what is wrong with that girl?"

I say something like, "Yeah," and get away as quickly as possible.

In gym we're doing volleyball. When I see Nelson, I think how weird it is that I just saw him in the supply room on Wednesday—and yet it feels like forever ago. I wonder if he knows about me and Declan. He must. He was in the gym when we started dancing.

I don't know why that makes me feel bad.

At one point I'm rotated out at the same time as Nelson is. We're both sitting on the sidelines, but on opposite sides of the net because we're on different teams.

I raise my hand, wave a little. But he doesn't wave back.

I always clean up in the bathroom after gym. As I'm washing my face, I hear the door open, a burst of laughter.

Then a familiar voice saying loudly, "Oh, my God, I can't use this bathroom. Smells like something *died* in here. Uck, excuse me."

As she leaves, I think how Marnie always overdoes things. She tries to sound like Alexa, but it never works. She's just not cool enough to pull it off.

I splash water on my face, tell myself I don't care.

But as I walk downstairs to chorus at the end of the day, I feel myself getting mad. Every step, I stomp a little harder. So, Alexa is all mad at me? Fine. She thinks I have no right to be with Declan? Fine. Elissa only wants to talk to me because I'm with Declan? Fine. Nelson *won't* talk to me because I'm with Declan? Fine. I don't care anymore. I just don't care. Maybe the whole school has gone insane, but I do not have to. . . .

I am almost at the practice room when I hear Declan call out, "Hey, Anna."

I'm in such a bad mood, I almost yell, *What*? But then I see his face. It's worried, nervous. I have this strange thought that he really doesn't know how cute he is—and that that's something I really like about him.

He pulls me to one side, says, "Did something weird happen in the cafeteria?"

With that one question, all the evil that's been churning around in my stomach disappears. "Uh, yeah. Weird, but no big deal."

"Like . . . she actually shoved you?"

"Yeah, but . . . I don't know. Maybe she was really into getting that last cheeseburger."

He laughs. I love that I made him laugh. But then he says, "That's messed up. You're okay, right?"

"Totally."

"Do you want to hang? After school or something? I feel really bad about this."

"Why should you feel bad?"

The rest of the chorus is arriving. I hear Bridget say, "Hey, guys," and I get self-conscious—isn't there anywhere in this school you can be alone?

In a lower voice I say, "Definitely, let's do something."

And, I swear, I sing a little better in chorus that afternoon.

Afterward, I race up to my locker to get my stuff. Eve comes by as I'm stuffing books into my bag and says, "Whoa, no rush. The show doesn't start until four thirty."

Oops. Totally forgot algebra and *Dumb, Rich, and*

Famous. For a second I think, *You have to go down and tell Declan you can't meet him. That you made a date with Eve and—*

But homework with Eve isn't a date. And it's something we can do anytime. This is my first *date* date with Declan.

So I say, "Please don't kill me."

Eve frowns. "What?"

"Just, Declan asked if I wanted to do something after school. He's all upset because of the Alexa thing. And I feel like it's important because . . ."

But I don't really know why it would be important, other than to show Alexa she didn't break us up. I only know I really, really want to go.

Eve nods slowly. "So no math homework and no *Dumb, Rich, and Famous*."

"Can we do it tomorrow?"

"It's due tomorrow."

I say, "Oh." Think: *Then why didn't you ask me for help earlier?*

But that's jerky. If I'm breaking a date with Eve, I have no right to criticize her. If she says this is a drag, I will break the date with Declan. It will suck—but that's what I'll do.

But Eve shrugs, says, "No biggie. Another D won't kill me."

I want to hug her for being so sweet. Zipping up my book bag, I say, "Let me know what happens on *Dumb, Rich, and Famous.*"

"Sure. Maybe I'll call Syd, see if she wants to watch."

I say, "Yeah," even though I hate the idea of Eve and Syd doing something without me. "I'm meeting Declan outside, you want to . . . ?"

"Three's a triangle. Be good—not."

She smiles. I smile back.

It feels sad anyway.

I turn, go downstairs to meet Declan.

NINE

THE PAGE OF WANDS
*Kind, loyal,
trustworthy . . . a dark young man*

A week later I am sitting in my room when my mom knocks. When I say, "Come in," she says, "Oh, you're off the phone."

I nod, wondering why she didn't just pick it up if that was what she wanted to know.

Then she says, "You've been on a lot lately."

"Yeah." I know what my mom is asking. I also know I don't want to tell her.

She waits for a moment, then says, "Well, remember that other people live in this house too, okay?"

I say, "I will," even as I think, *Excuse me, when do I not remember that? A few phone calls, and all of a sudden, I'm the evil, selfish one?*

It's really weird. You can go through your whole life being nice to people, and then the one time you have your own thing, everybody freaks out. It's like, *Wait*, you're *not supposed to have a life*.

Because it's not just my mom. The other day Syd e-mailed me: *Is Russell making crank calls? I keep getting a busy signal. Call me, okay?* When I did, she said, "What's *up*?" like I'd been on the phone forever.

I said, "I was talking to Declan."

"I guess the boy likes to talk."

I almost said, *Well, he likes to talk to me, Sydney*. But I didn't. Just asked, "So, what's up?"

And what was it, this big thing she had to talk to me about? The thing that could not wait? Calling Tatiana's owner this Friday. Which, okay, yes, is important. But not an emergency.

And *Eve*. Lately, I don't even want to be around her. She's got something to say about every little thing I do. *You're wearing that? You're doing what? You said hi to whom?*

I'm not kidding. The other day we saw Chris Abernathy, and he said "Yo" to me as he went by. Now, I don't like Chris, but I wasn't going to be obnoxious, so I said "Hey."

That's it, "Hey." Not *I love you, you're a god* or anything like that. Just "Hey."

To Eve, it was like I had locked lips with Satan. "Okay, first Elissa Maxwell, now Chris Abernathy? What's going on with you? What happened to Operation Freak Victory?"

What I didn't say was, *It's not about Operation Freak Victory. It's about Declan. And me.*

Not . . . you.

And to be totally honest, I think it's cool that people are into me and Declan. It's like when the cards first predicted it; some other power saying, *Yes, this is right. You two belong together.* With Alexa giving me the evil eye every time she sees me and Marnie treating me like toxic waste, it's a relief to know that not everybody hates my guts.

The one small drag is that people always look for Declan when they see me. I can see girls are disappointed when they come up to say hi and he's not there. Also confused. Like, *Why aren't you guys ever together?*

I still like Declan's rule. No PDA. No couply stuff. It's just a drag sometimes, that's all.

On the other hand, Eve and I no longer have to fight for a decent seat in the cafeteria. People have started making room for us at the good tables. Not Subzero, but I wouldn't want to sit there anyway. Not with Alexa, thank you.

One day as we sit down, Eve says, "I think it's cool Declan doesn't sit in Subzero. Well, except when Alexa made him."

"Yeah, he's cool that way."

"Although . . ."—she looks around—". . . where does he eat?"

I bite into my tuna sandwich. "What do you mean?"

"I never see him. Doesn't he eat lunch anymore?"

I drink some milk while I think of what to say. Eve's question seems simple. I could explain that Declan eats earlier than I do—partly because I want to keep having lunch with her, and what does she think about that? But when she says, "Doesn't he eat lunch anymore?" what she's really saying is, *He ate lunch with Alexa, so how come he's not eating with you?*

Or even, *Are you guys actually going out or what? Because you sure don't act like you're going out.*

I look over at the über-cool section. All those girls on Zoe's list, those most likely to date Declan. If Declan were dating one of them, would he be so into the noncouple thing?

Then Eve says, "Oh, hey, Syd says this Friday, come over to her place, call the cat person, then pig out on pizza. Cool?"

I say, "Yeah, cool." But I'm still thinking about

what Eve said, the questions she was really asking.

And if I have the answers or not.

Every night Declan calls around eight o'clock. Usually, we're done with dinner by then. But tonight Russell decides he hates peas, and my mom insists that no one can leave the table until Russell has eaten ten peas. I point out that I have eaten all my peas and shouldn't be held hostage to Russell's stupid games. My mom says we stay at the table until everyone's done. It's a family rule.

I mutter, "Since when?" but my mom pretends not to hear.

When the phone rings at eight, I watch my mom to see if she'll get it. But she's busy separating out ten peas on Russell's plate, showing him how little he has to eat.

I say, "That's probably for me."

"Well, whoever it is can leave a message."

But I don't want Declan leaving a message. I don't want him to call and me not answer. Plus, if he leaves a message, my mom will hear it and say, *Who is this? I don't know this person.* I jump out of my chair, get to the phone just before the machine picks up.

My mom says, "Anna, I said—"

"I know, I'll come back the second I'm done,

okay?" My mom looks at Russell. She knows she can't fight him and me at the same time, so she says, "Five minutes."

I race back to my room, wait for the click that says my mom's hung up in the kitchen. Then I say, "Hey, sorry."

"What was all that?" asks Declan.

"Oh, my mom being lame about dinner. Thou shalt not leave the table until annoying son has eaten the peas of the land."

"God. I eat dinner with my mom. She always wants to talk to me. 'How was your day? What did you do? Talk to me so we don't notice Dad's working late again and I can feel like we're a normal family.'"

I laugh. "Yeah, it's like, 'Maybe that's your big thing, but leave me out of it.'"

"Definitely."

We start talking about other stuff—TV, school, psycho teachers. I love talking to Declan. Lately, I feel like he's the only person I can say anything to. He doesn't expect me to be nice all the time. And unlike some people, he won't go, *Why are you talking to Declan all the time?* Or, *Why* aren't *you talking to Declan?*

On impulse, I say, "Hey, what are you doing for lunch tomorrow?"

He hesitates, then says, "Uh, eating?"

"Do you want to . . . eat together? As in same time? Same table even?"

There's a long pause. Declan says, "Whoa, same table. I don't know if I can handle that."

I can't tell if he's kidding, if I'm pushing him to do something he's not into.

I start to say, "You know what, forget it—" when Declan interrupts with, "But, yeah, okay."

I'm about to say *Great* when my mom throws open the door.

"Anna—off the phone. *Now.*"

On the way to school on Wednesday, I ask myself why I want to have lunch with Declan. I do not want to show him off. There will be no nibbling on ears. But if we don't do stuff so people can watch and say, *Ooh, look,* we shouldn't not do stuff because people might watch and say, *Ooh, look.*

Besides, it serves Eve the tiniest bit right if she doesn't have anyone to eat with. When she says, "I have to talk to Fegelson after class, so can we go to lunch a little later?" I get a kick out of telling her, "That's okay. I'm having lunch with Dec today."

Eve shrugs. "So—all three."

I don't say anything.

She stares at me. "What? I can't have lunch with you if the great Declan is present?"

I don't know what to say. *Well, no, you can't. Lunch with Declan isn't lunch, it's a date. And you don't have your friend along on a date.*

Eve says, "You're serious. I can't have lunch with you."

I never thought she'd make a big thing of it. This is now no longer fun. I say, "Just not . . . this lunch."

"Man, I can't believe it. Since when are you like *this?*"

"Like *what*, Eve?"

"Little Miss Oh, I Have a Boyfriend."

Which is so unfair, I almost scream. I have tried so hard not to be like that, and yet the second I want to have lunch alone with Declan, I'm supposedly Little Miss I Have a Boyfriend.

And I wouldn't have even wanted to have lunch with him if Eve hadn't made me feel bad about *not* having lunch with him.

I want to shout, *You're trying to make me feel like I'm acting all superior because I have a boyfriend. But you always act superior to me, you always act like you're the one it's about. And you can't stand it that someone else is getting attention for a change.*

I don't say it—but I don't have to. Eve knows me, she knows what I'm thinking.

Well, good. Let her see I'm not backing down this time.

"Okay," she says quietly, and goes off to class by herself.

What I hate about fights is that I get obsessed. The whole morning I play and replay the argument with Eve in my head, thinking up things I should have said. Sometimes I'm more hurtful, other times I'm nicer.

Maybe at lunchtime I'll try to call Syd. She is very wise about fights with Eve.

Then I remember, *Oh, right, I can't. Having lunch with Declan.*

He's waiting for me outside the lunchroom. He's wearing his bulky army jacket, and his hair is flopping perfectly over his face. As always, his hands are in his pockets, but he smiles when he sees me. Then he goes through the cafeteria doors. After a moment I follow.

As we wait on line, Declan says, "Sorry about the phone last night. I hope your mom wasn't pissed."

"Don't worry about it," I say hastily. The last thing I want is for Declan to stop calling because he thinks it might annoy my mother.

As Declan gets his noodles, he says, "Just, my mom has no friends, so I don't think about tying up the phone at my house."

"My mom doesn't talk to a lot of people either," I assure him. "She just wanted to bust my chops."

We find a table in the middle and sit down. People are craning their heads to look at us, like we're a TV show or something. I hate to admit it, but I like sitting here with Declan. Not that I want to be one of the cool people. But it's nice to be one of the okay people for a change. One of the people who's accepted and doesn't have to worry.

I look at Declan, think, *This is it. What the cards predicted.* I can't believe it actually came true.

I don't want it to look like I'm staring at him, so I glance at his book bag. He has some books out from the library. One of them's on the *Titanic*. I love the *Titanic*. I've seen the movies a hundred times, even the old ones.

I say, "You like *Titanic*?"

He nods over his noodles. "Disasters in general. I'm really into the *Hindenburg* right now, but *Titanic*'s interesting."

"There's some show on the *Titanic* coming up on TV. They're going down and taking pictures of it before it disintegrates."

Declan looks up from his noodles. "Oh, yeah? When's it on?"

I try to remember. "Friday, I think?"

Declan nods. Then says, "You want to watch it at my house?"

There's something about Friday that tickles my brain, something I'm supposed to remember. But I can't remember, so it can't be that important. I say, "Yeah, that'd be . . ."

I'm trying to think of exactly how I should define what this would be—awesome? okay?—when I hear Chris Abernathy laugh.

It's a mean laugh, an "I'm gonna get you" laugh. Instinctively, I look to make sure I'm not the victim . . . and that's when I see Nelson.

He's sitting in the Subzero Zone.

He probably didn't have a choice. The cafeteria's jammed. But some kids sit on the floor rather than break the rule. Nelson's so out of it, he may not have even noticed. But Chris did.

I think, *Leave him alone, leave him alone, leave him alone. . . .*

Then Chris says in a loud voice, "Hey, Kyle, what causes brain damage?"

Kyle thinks a moment. "Certain drugs . . . too

much vodka . . . your mom dropping you on your head when you're a baby . . ."

"Yeah, yeah!" Chris looks at Nelson again. "That gives you kind of a flat head, doesn't it? Like, you always know retards 'cause of the shape of their head."

Nelson is eating his sandwich in little tiny bites, like he has no clue anyone's talking about him. But he has to know. He has to hear. Everyone else can hear.

And they're starting to laugh. Not loud, but a little bit. I look over at Declan. He's balling his napkin up in his fist.

Chris goes on. "Yeah, their heads are all squished on top. And they walk kind of slow. And they talk . . . like . . . this." He does a slow, halting voice, just like Nelson when he's nervous.

I say to Declan, "This is so wrong."

Declan drops his napkin on the table. "Ignore it."

I'm about to say, *Ignore it?* when I hear Chris say loudly, "Man, I hate retards. They freak me out."

"You never know when they're going to snap," says Kyle.

"School shouldn't allow them here with us sane, normal types."

Real laughter over that one; primarily because everyone knows Chris is not sane or normal.

"Ban retards, I say!" yells Chris.

"Lock 'em up," shouts Kyle.

"Man, let's just kill 'em." Chris gets up, holds out his notebook to Lindsey Pierce at the next table. "Miss, would you sign my petition for the extermination of retards?" Lindsey's laughing, but she shakes her head. Chris holds it out to Tara Birch. "How about you, miss?"

"Come on, Tar, sign it!" says Kyle.

You can tell Tara wasn't going to sign it, but now that Kyle's paying attention to her, she grins and picks up a pen.

Then Lindsey says, "Oh, why not?" and signs. Then the girl next to her takes the book.

"Stand up for your rights," shouts Chris as more and more people take the notebook. "Take back your school! Down with retards!"

I don't know what to do. The whole thing is getting out of control. Nelson is still quietly eating his sandwich, but the fact that he's one of the few people ignoring Chris means he knows exactly who Chris is talking about. He's reading his book, *The Greatest Graphic Novel Ever*.

I say to Declan, "We have to do something."

Who shakes his head. "Uh, no way."

I don't get it. How can he just sit there and do

nothing? But then I remember Declan when Zoe dubbed him "NerdBoy," tortured by the likes of Chris and Kyle. The tripping, the flipped trays. "Hey, Ark-Ark! Intruders present!"

No wonder he doesn't want to get in their face.

Then Chris walks over to Nelson, holds out the notebook. I hold my breath as Chris says, "Care to see how many people want you exterminated, retard?"

In my head I scream, *You're disgusting!* but I never get a chance to scream it for real. Because now Nelson is screaming. Screaming and throwing things.

He takes his tray, hurls it at Chris. Grabs his jacket, throws it in his face. Then he takes the notebook itself and starts swinging it at Chris's head.

Then everyone starts screaming, and finally, finally, the stupid cafeteria monitors wake up and decide to do something.

Here's what they do. To Chris and Kyle, they do nothing. No punishment at all.

Nelson is suspended.

The next day everyone is talking about the fight and Nelson's suspension. Everyone thinks it's about time. Everyone thinks, *Poor Chris and Kyle—it was just a* joke.

Maybe suspension is no big deal in some schools, but it is in ours. People hardly ever get suspended, and when they are, it's for a day, maybe two. But Nelson got suspended for more than that. That says *We're not sure you belong here.* A week says, *We'll use any excuse to get rid of you.*

And what's really awful is that a few months ago, I wouldn't have cared. I probably would have said, *Yeah, well, Nelson is pretty scary.*

I wish I had his phone number, so I could make sure he's okay.

Normally, Eve and I would avoid each other after an argument like the one we had over the Declan lunch. But we're both so angry about Nelson's getting the shaft while Chris and Kyle are off the hook, it's like we never fought.

In study hall I say, "I can't believe it."

Eve says, "What about it can't you believe?"

"That they think it's all Nelson's fault. Don't they know what jerks Chris and Kyle are?"

Eve rolls her eyes. "Are you kidding? Like they care."

Maybe it's stupid of me, but I can't help thinking that the school might care if they knew the truth about Chris Abernathy. They've got Nelson down as a "problem,"—but it's Chris who's the real maniac. Only Chris wears nice clothes, has his hair cut the right way—and because he looks right, nobody looks too closely, so he doesn't get caught.

Then I hear Eve say, "So, we're on for tomorrow, right?"

Having no idea what she's talking about, I say carefully, "Tomorrow."

"Meeting with Syd? Calling the last cat person, saving felines, all that jazz?"

Friday. Syd's plan—that's what I forgot when I made the date with Declan. But the Declan date is a TV program; Syd's is a phone call, and we can do that anytime.

I say, "Tomorrow's no good."

"What?" Eve slumps. "Oh, don't tell me—Mom needs you."

"No, that's not it. It's . . ." This should be good news, fun news. "It's just Declan asked me out."

There's a long, ugly pause. Then Eve says flatly, "And Friday is, like, the only day you can possibly see him."

I don't dare tell Eve about the *Titanic* show; she'll laugh me off the planet. "Can't we do Saturday instead?"

"No. Syd's going to her grandmother's."

I'm about to start throwing out days—Monday, Tuesday, any day—when Eve stands abruptly and says, "If you can't do it, you have to tell Syd yourself, okay? Because I won't."

"I didn't ask you to."

"Good. Because this was actually somewhat important to her."

I can't believe Eve is trying to make me feel guilty about Syd. Like she hasn't been insensitive to her a million times. Like she ever cared about the cats the way Syd and I did.

This isn't about me breaking a date at all, I think. *This is about* why *I'm breaking the date.* Which is not fair.

"I'll call her," I say.

And I do, the second I get home. As I dial, I think it's good to call Syd when I'm still angry at Eve. Otherwise, I'd probably be thinking, *Oh, should I cancel with Declan? I did say I'd do it, it's rotten to bag out.* Now, all I can think is, *No, for once, I am not changing my plans.*

That is, until I hear Syd say, "So, whose house are we doing for tomorrow?"

"Uh, that's actually the thing. I can't do tomorrow."

Normally, Syd would say something like, *Oh, man, that sucks. How about Saturday?*

But she doesn't. She doesn't say anything. Which, in Syd-speak, means, *I am majorly pissed off.*

"I am really sorry."

Automatically, Syd says, "No, that's . . ." But she can't quite do the "okay."

"Can we do it Sunday when you get back from your grandmother's?"

"Not really. I wanted . . . Look, never mind, we'll do it another time."

"Next week, we can do it next week."

"Whatever," says Syd. "Maybe I'll just do it myself."

The thought of Syd searching for Tat all on her own is so lonely, I'm about to say, *You know what, let's do Friday like we planned.*

But then Syd says, "Or else me and Eve'll just do it. Look, I have to go. Talk to you later, okay? Bye."

Later that night I call Syd again. But her phone is busy. So is Eve's. I wonder if they're talking about me, what a jerk I'm being.

God, I can't believe her.

I know. She's pathetic.

What, she can never say no?

It's like anything he wants, she does, just to stay with him.

To distract myself, I go into the living room to find my mom watching one of those goofy movies about women with crazy husbands or crazy kids. Seeing me, she smiles, says, "Come on in, honey."

Finally, a person not horrified to see me. I sit down next to my mom on the couch.

Then the commercial comes on. Mom clicks on the mute button and says, "Oh, I forgot to tell you, they canceled Russell's judo class tomorrow afternoon, so he'll be coming home with you."

I look up at my mom. "I have plans."

My mom looks up. "What plans?"

"I'm . . ." If I tell my mom about Declan, she will immediately say, *No way.* Anything having to do with guys, she's ten times as strict as usual. "I'm supposed to go out with some friends."

"Can't they come over here?"

Hey, Declan, come over and help me babysit my putrid brother. "Not really. We were thinking of seeing a movie."

"Well, I'm sorry, honey. I don't know what else to do."

"Can't he go to Dad's?"

"Your dad has some appointment he can't get out of."

"What about a friend's? What about goopy Teddy?"

"Teddy's in Florida." She smiles, sees I'm not smiling back. "I'm sorry, Anna. I'll make it up to you, I swear."

"No, you won't," I say flatly. "I'm not doing it."

"Anna . . ."

"No, forget it." The fact that this didn't have to be like this—if my mom just had half a brain and remembered to call someone, anyone—makes me furious. Sometimes I feel like she gets away with being a big fat dip because she thinks, *Oh, it's okay, Anna will do it.*

Well, Anna isn't doing it. Not this time. I've screwed up too much to back down now.

My mom takes a deep breath. "What if I promise I'll be home by five thirty and you can go meet your friends then?"

"No." I fold my arms, stare at the soundless TV.

"Anna, work with me a little here, please."

"No."

It's the magic word. There is absolutely nothing my mother can say to it—partly because she knows she's wrong, partly because I have never done this before and she doesn't have a clue how to handle it. I know I'm being a pain, and frankly, I like being a pain. Like, *No, I'm not always going to be your good little Anna who just does whatever you tell her to do.*

Quietly, she asks, "Who are these friends you're seeing?"

Oh, no. No way. You "have" to work. Dad has "some appointment." You guys get to be all vague about why you can't take care of Russell, but I have to be completely specific? He's your stupid kid, I want to scream. *You take care of him.*

"Some friends from school."

"Do I know them?"

"I don't remember."

It would be very easy to lie, to say, *Yeah, you remember Bridget from chorus.* My mom would never call Bridge's parents to check, the way she might call Eve's or Syd's. But I don't want to lie. I want to tell my mother I have things I want to do too, and those things are important—whether she approves of them or not.

My mom says, "You don't remember."

"Yeah, like maybe at some school thing you might have met them."

"What are their names?"

Oh, God, she is so pissing me off. "What does it matter?"

"Anna! What are their names?"

I know exactly what she's doing. She's making this be about where I'm going and who I'm with instead of what it really is about, which is that she's a disorganized mess who expects me to do everything.

Which is why I say, "It doesn't matter what their names are."

"Oh, yes, it—"

"No, it doesn't. What matters is that I am not taking care of Russell tomorrow and that's final. I don't have to give you a reason. You never give me one."

"That is *not* true," says my mom. "You absolutely know the reason."

I sneer. "Oh, yeah. For Dad, it's work. Or an appointment. Or a baseball game. With you, it's work or a friend. Or a meeting. Your life, in other words. Well, guess what? I have a life too, and it doesn't cease to exist whenever you feel like it. So find someone else to babysit, I'm not doing it!"

I storm back to my room before my mom can say anything else. As I do, I see Russell standing at the door to his bedroom. His eyes are huge, and he's clutching Bruce. We must have woken him up by yelling.

My parents did that once. I guess they waited until we were both in bed to start screaming at each other. I don't know why, because we heard everything they said. I was sitting up in bed when the door opened, and there was Russell with Bruce the First. I gestured for him to come in, and he shut the door and clambered up on my bed. And for a while we just sat there— me, Russell, and Bruce. I remember I wanted to be as quiet as possible. Like it was wrong that we were listening in somehow and that if my parents found out, they'd scream at us instead. Russell didn't say a word the whole time. But I could hear him breathing.

Now, for a split second, I feel sorry for Russell. Then I think, *No*. Yanking open my bedroom door, I go into my room, then slam the door shut.

TEN

TEN OF SWORDS
Burden, misery, heartache

Friday morning, my mom coolly informs me that she will be taking the afternoon off in order to take care of Russell. I say, "Great"—like it has nothing to do with me.

Russell is very quiet on the way to school. At one point I say, "Hey, Russell, what animal are you today?"

He mumbles, "Not any."

For a moment I think of saying, *Let's be penguins.* But Russell doesn't look too into being anything today. I guess he's still upset about the fight.

I am not upset about the fight I had with my mom because, frankly, it's about time I stood up to her. But I am worried about Eve. Technically, we're not in a fight. But I know she's mad at me for canceling on Syd.

I'll know where we stand if she's not waiting on the steps. If Eve is mad at you, she's very good at not being around.

But she's there. I can't believe how relieved I am to see her. Figuring it's best to get it out in the open, I say, "I talked to Syd."

"Yeah, she told me." From Eve's tone, it doesn't sound like Syd told her anything good.

But as we walk inside, she says, "So tonight's the big night, huh? Your big date?"

"Yeah. It's no—" I want to tell her it's no big deal, but you don't bail on your friends for no big deal.

There's so much I want to talk to Eve about. Like, what do you do when you go to a guy's house? What do you not do? Because I don't have any clear thought on that. Up to now, the sum total of my romantic experience has been pressing mouths with David Farkis during *E.T.* at camp.

But I can't talk to her because, somehow, whenever we talk about Declan, we end up fighting.

I say, "You know . . ." just as Eve says, "Hey . . ."

We both stop. I say, "You go."

Eve looks up at the ceiling like she's reconsidering. Then she says, "Call me tomorrow. Give me the scoop, you know?"

I smile. "Definitely."

And we leave it there, while it's still okay.

In study period I try to get started on my English paper. We had three choices: "Discuss the connection between freedom and nature in *As You Like It*." Or "talk about how Mark Twain uses superstition in *Tom Sawyer*." Or "was Oedipus responsible for his fate?" Which, in a moment of madness, I chose. You can say yes or no, but you have to make an argument either way. Frankly, I wish Ms. Taramini had told us to write either yes or no, because I don't have a clue if he's responsible or not. But Ms. Taramini's not into being clear any more than she's into being nice or even remotely human. I have definitely decided I am in the Hate Ms. Taramini camp.

At the top of the page I write, *Was Oedipus Responsible for His Fate?*

I think for a moment. Write, *Yes.*

I think some more. Then I get a drink of water.

Come back, tear the page out of my notebook. Start over.

Was Oedipus Responsible for His Fate? No.

Then *Yes.*

Then *No* again.

Then *Who cares?*

I put my pen down, start thinking about my out-fit. I tried on a million things to get the right look for this date. I'm still not sure I got it. These days, I never really feel like I look right—and yet I spend a lot more time thinking about it than I ever did before.

I'm just wondering if I can duck home for a quick change when I see Chris and Kyle come into the library. Chris has a little bruise near his eye, where Nelson socked him. He gives me a nod. I don't nod back. All I can think of is how unfair it is that they're still in school while Nelson's not. There's already a rumor that the school has asked Nelson's mother to send him somewhere else next year.

Chris and Kyle have sat down. But they're not studying. Instead, they're flicking spitballs at some girls. Some girls would like that, but these girls don't. One of them glares, but Chris snickers, flicks another spitball.

The girl who glared says, "Cut it out." Chris mimics her: "Cut it out." He throws a pen at her.

These are the people the school has decided are okay. The good people, the normal ones, the nonfreaks.

Someone should do something.

Correction: *I* should do something.

Only I don't know what. Start a petition to end Nelson's suspension? Yeah, a lot of people would sign that. Force Chris and Kyle to admit they're jerks? Another real likely possibility.

But there has to be something.

I'm still thinking about what that something might be when I meet Declan after school. As we take the bus across town to his house, I tell him about Chris and Kyle in the library. I expect him to be outraged, but he just shrugs.

Then I say, "I can't believe Nelson got suspended and those creeps didn't."

He snorts. "What can't you believe? Nelson's a maniac."

"It wasn't his fault."

"No, it's not his *fault*, it's just . . ." He hunkers down, shoves his hands in his pockets. "That's not how you deal with that stuff."

I want to say, *Really? Because at the time, I felt like throwing a few trays, so I can totally relate.*

Getting off the bus, I say, "Don't you think Chris and Kyle should have been punished too?"

"Yeah, like that's going to happen."

Then before I can say anything more, he stops in front of a building and points. *"Mi casa."*

Maybe because Declan says his dad works all the time and they live on the East Side, I thought his place would be really big and fancy. And it is fancy, but it's not . . . nice. The furniture is rich-looking, but there's too much of it. It belongs in a bigger house. The place is silent. It feels cramped and empty at the same time.

Declan points: "Living room, kitchen, hallway, parents' room, my room. Oh, bathroom opposite my room. That's it, the big tour. Want something to drink?" He goes to the kitchen and opens the fridge. "It's water, juice, or Coke."

"Juice is good." I look around, hoping to see a dog or a cat, something friendly. Declan hands me a glass. "So, what's your room like?"

"Right this way . . ."

As we walk down the hall, I wonder if Alexa ever came over to his house. If she asked to see his room. Then I wonder if his room will look like the old Declan or the new Declan?

It's neither. What it is, is very, very neat. You can see on the walls that there used to be posters, but they're gone. The bookshelves mostly have school-books on them, except for a few old science fiction paperbacks. The bed is made, there's no mess on his bureau. On his chair there's a T-shirt for some band I never heard of. But it's laid so neatly over the back of the chair, it makes me wonder if Declan put it there specially for me to see it.

"Wow, my mom would love you. You're like Mr. Neat."

"Not really. I got rid of a lot of stuff over the summer, so there's not that much to get messy."

I smile. "Time to get new stuff."

"Don't know what."

There's something a little sad about that. Looking for something else to talk about, I check out his books. There's a big, battered book called *Disaster!* It looks old-fashioned but really cool, and I bet it has a chapter on *Titanic*. Without thinking, I say, "Hey, can I borrow this?"

He hesitates, then says, "Sure. I haven't looked at it in a while."

Then I find last year's yearbook underneath some textbooks. I pull it out and open it up, but Declan says, "Oh, man, I thought I got rid of that."

"You can't get rid of *yearbooks*." I flip to the back to see who signed. Almost all the pages are empty. One note from Dmitri Cortezar: *Stay sane, dude!*

Declan takes the book out of my hands. "Seriously."

"I want to see your picture."

"No, you don't."

"Come on, my picture reeks too."

"No, it doesn't." He opens his closet, puts the book inside. "Come on, let's go see what's on."

The *Titanic* show isn't on until six o'clock and it's only four thirty. For a while we flick around the channels. At one point we find *Ovidian Planet*—although not a scene with Ark-Ark, thank God.

Declan says, "I hate that show. The effects are terrible," and clicks to the next channel.

We're sitting on the couch. It is very hard not to be aware that no one else is home, that we're all alone. When I sat down, I tried to pick a spot that was not too far from Declan, but not too close, either. If I sat too close, it'd be like declaring *Make-out time!* and I don't know if I want to declare that. On the other hand, I definitely want it to be an option.

Declan is slouching with his legs stretched out, eyes fixed on the TV. If he's thinking what I'm thinking, it doesn't show. Maybe he's not. Only I kind of wish he was. It's like, *Hi, I'm here! Yeah, I see you. Not interested.*

I think of the Queen of Wands, the card that showed how I see myself. A total nice girl. Kind, devoted, chaste . . .

Hmm, maybe that's why Declan's on the other side of the couch.

But if he's not thinking of doing anything, I don't want him to know I am, so I say, "Do you think we should do something to help Nelson?"

He frowns at the TV. "Like what?"

"I don't know. Find out if Ms. Kenworthy knows what really happened. Because you know what I bet? I bet Chris and Kyle backed up each other's stories, but no one told Nelson's side."

Declan shrugs. "I'm sure she knows. I'm sure she doesn't care."

I think about that for a moment. Eve would say the same thing: Teachers don't care. The school doesn't care. It has certain people marked as okay and certain people marked as freaks, and nothing will change that. If you're okay, you can get away with a lot. If you're a freak, forget it. And if it's freak versus okay, guess who wins?

But I don't think Ms. Kenworthy is like that. I think she doesn't know how things really are at Eberly. I mean, how can she be all about fairness and world peace and not care about what goes on at her own school?

"Well, I think we should go to Ms. Kenworthy and make sure she knows."

"Knows *what*?" Declan clicks again.

"That Chris and Kyle were calling Nelson a retard. That they were handing around a petition saying he should be exterminated."

"Uh, yeah, and when Chris and Kyle get suspended

and they find out who told, how's that going to be?"

"Who cares?" Because I know what Declan means—if they do find out, it won't be fun. But you can't not do something because you're scared. You have to at least pretend you're not frightened of bullies—otherwise, they totally win.

"Besides," I say, "maybe we won't ask her to punish Chris and Kyle. Just end Nelson's suspension and . . . I don't know, apologize or something."

"Why? I bet Nelson's thrilled to be suspended. I would be."

"No, you wouldn't. Not if everyone said you were a freak and you deserved it."

That hits home, I can tell. Declan's quiet for a moment. Then he says, "You can do it; I don't want to."

Then it's my turn to be quiet. I really thought Declan would do this with me, that he would see why it was so important.

As if he knows I'm disappointed, Declan says, "Guy's such a dork."

I want to say to Declan, *We were all dorks not too long ago. I know I was. And, by the way, so were you . . . big-time. Yes, we're cool now, we're okay. But we don't side with people who are nasty to kids who are, hello, dorks just like we were.*

I try, "It's better if it's both of us. Two people saying the same thing is more believable. Otherwise, Ms. Kenworthy's just going to think I'm his friend sticking up for him."

"Right—but I'm not Nelson's friend. I don't know why you think I am."

He says it in this fierce voice, a voice that tells me how important it is to him that he's not Nelson's friend. He's Declan now, not sad, pathetic Ark-Ark. And he's not going to screw that up by having anything to do with the school's official loser—especially if it means defying Chris and Kyle, who, if they wanted to, could turn him back into Ark-Ark in a second. All it would take is one tipped tray in the lunchroom.

Which I get. I really do. And part of me feels bad for Declan.

But the other part of me wants to say, *You can't let them win like that. They're not gods who decide everything in your life. They don't say who you are. . . .*

Declan would say, *But they do tell everyone else who you are. And that does decide your fate—at Eberly, anyway.*

Then I think of Eve. A lot of people think she's strange. Like Zoe calling her "GoofyGothGrl." But she doesn't care. She'd never do something or not do it based on what people might say. And that's why she might be a freak, but she's never been a victim. No one would dare tip her tray.

I say, "Well, I'm going to talk to Ms. Kenworthy."

"Fine," says Declan shortly.

We don't talk at all while the show is on—not even during the commercials. It's a boring show. All they talk about is the ship itself, how it was built, and what happened when the iceberg hit. There are all these computer graphics showing the side of the ship being ripped open. Then they show you how the watertight compartments were flooded and all the rest of the technical blah-blah.

What's so weird about the *Titanic* is how sure they were. Nobody thought the ship could sink. They thought they'd taken every precaution imaginable, that there was no way anything bad could happen. That's why there weren't enough lifeboats, because they were so certain nothing could sink the *Titanic*. They'd done everything right.

That was their one mistake: being so sure that they hadn't made one.

My mom is waiting for me in the kitchen when I get home. The last time she did that was when Mrs. Rosemont died, and I wonder if she has bad news. Then I remember: We're fighting.

As I take off my coat and put it in the hall closet, she says, "How was the movie?"

"It was okay."

"What did you see?"

"Some dumb action thing."

I approach the entrance of the kitchen but don't go in. My mom asks, "What on earth made you pick that?"

"Bridget heard it was good."

"Oh, you went with Bridget?" Rats. I forgot I wasn't going to tell my mom who I went with. Then she says casually, "She doesn't strike me as a girl who's big into action flicks."

I'm thinking how I can connect Bridget and action movies when my mom stands up and says, "You know, what bothers me, Anna, is not that I had to leave work early today. What bothers me—really bothers me—is that you're lying to me and I don't know why."

My mother doesn't yell. She doesn't shout. She just sounds sad. I remember how good it felt to be mad at her last night, to throw "No" in her face again and again. I wish I could be mad at her now. Because now all I feel is awful.

I want to explain to her that I'm not lying to her because I'm doing something so terrible. But part of the reason I *am* lying to her is that I don't want her to know everything about my life. I don't want to hear, *Oh, my God, you have a boyfriend, who is he, when can I meet him?* Because somehow that makes me a little girl again, and I'm sick of that. I'm sick of being the girl she can always count on, the one she never has to worry about. My mom always says I'm a "good kid." Well, I'm sick of being a good kid.

My mother is watching me, waiting for me to confess, to say I'm sorry, to turn back into her great girl, her good kid. And part of me wants to. But I don't want to give her Declan and me. Somehow I want that to be secret from her, out of her reach.

But I do say, "I'm sorry."

She sighs. "I'm sorry too."

I don't know what else to say—great, we're both sorry—so I go back to my room. I look for Mouli, then remember today is Friday. He belongs to Russell on Fridays, so he must be in his room. Probably prefers it there. I tell myself I don't care. I have tried everything to get that stupid cat to like me. Nothing works, so forget him.

Sitting down on my bed, I get out my notebook and start making a list of everything I want to say to Ms. Kenworthy to get her to see how ridiculous it is that she's always going on about justice when she lets injustice go on in her own school. As I write, it turns into a kind of letter to her. Maybe if I chicken out and can't speak in front of her, I'll just hand her this.

I really wish Declan would come with me. Only he's not going to, so . . .

I wish he weren't so afraid of Chris and those guys. But he is, so . . .

And I wish he weren't mad at me for wanting to do this. Because I can tell he is.

Why?

I draw a circle around Nelson's name. I guess if you've just escaped the Freak Zone and you're dating someone who is definitely not a P&P, the last thing you want is for everyone to know you're helping the school's number one freak—and ratting out the head über-cool.

And you probably don't want your girlfriend doing it either.

I think of how Declan acted after I said I might talk to Ms. Kenworthy. I don't remember a thing he said, it was all bored "Yeahs" and shrugs. Like I could not possibly matter less. What will he do if I do see Ms. Kenworthy? Will he say, *Uh, sorry, I don't date freak fans?*

A small twist in my stomach: Should I not do this?

Nelson will never know if I don't. He's certainly not expecting me to. It's not like I told Eve or anyone else I was going to do it. The only person I told was Declan. Who would be just as happy if I said on

Monday, *Eh, you know what? Nelson's probably happier being suspended anyway. . . .*

So it's no big deal if I don't. And a slightly big deal if I do. It's one thing to have everyone talking about you when they think you're cool. It's another to have everyone talking about what a jerk you are.

What's the deal with her and Nelson? That's pretty odd, don't you think?

Immediately, I think, *Forget it. Not doing it.*

But then I remember Chris's face as he hurled the spitball at that girl. She asked him to stop, and he threw a pen at her. That's what guys like Chris do. And we all go around saying it's okay when it's not. And then I think of Nelson screaming in the lunchroom. How he was just sitting there, and for that, they wanted him exterminated. All those people who were laughing. When they don't even know him.

I pick up my pen and write, *You always say we should believe that what we do makes a difference. That we're not helpless. That if we can do something and we don't, we're not blameless, either.*

So that's why I'm here, Ms. Kenworthy. . . .

ELEVEN

THE TOWER

Ruin of all plans, unexpected disaster

I've been to the principal's office only once before, and that was in sixth grade, when we found our math teacher, Mr. Bradley, asleep on the classroom floor, and we were worried he might be dead. So the class picked me to go tell Ms. Kenworthy. He wasn't dead, but he didn't come back the next year, either.

A lot of people think Ms. Kenworthy is only interested in the kids with rich parents and getting good publicity for the school with things like Alexa's commercials. But she's always been nice to me, and my parents certainly aren't rich. She is a little stiff sometimes, and she hates when people disagree with her. Like once at a school assembly on smoking, Chris raised his hand and said it was his right to get cancer and die if he wanted to, and you could tell, she was seriously angry.

So she's probably not going to be thrilled when I tell her she was wrong to suspend Nelson.

As I raise my hand to knock on the door, I think, *This is stupid*. It's not like she's going to pick up the phone and say, *Nelson, come back! Anna has explained everything!* Adults never take you seriously enough to admit that they're wrong. So why get Ms. Kenworthy mad at me for nothing?

Because it isn't nothing. It's Nelson, and it's unjust, and I hate being in a place that's unjust. It makes me feel like an unjust person if I don't say anything.

Oh, so this is all about you wanting to be nice. Aren't you so great? Who made you Master of the Universe?

That almost stops me, because I hate it when people do things so people will notice and say, *She's so wonderful.*

But if I don't say anything, Nelson will stay suspended and everyone will think he's a maniac while Chris and Kyle are basically okay guys. And that's ridiculous.

Besides, I really think Ms. Kenworthy would want to know. I do think hearing what Chris and Kyle did will change the way she sees this.

I knock, hear "Come in."

I open the door, look in. "Is this an okay time?"

Ms. Kenworthy looks surprised but not horrified to see me. Waving me into her office, she says, "Yes, yes. Come in, Anna, sit down."

I do, feeling bad that she's being so nice to me when I'm about to tell her, *Uh, by the way, you were totally wrong....*

Ms. Kenworthy smiles. "What can I do for you?"

I fold my arms, then unfold them. "It's about the fight in the cafeteria." Ms. Kenworthy nods, but the smile definitely dims. "Just . . . I was there, and I saw what happened? And I really, really don't think Nelson should have been suspended."

Ms. Kenworthy is quiet for a moment, then says, "Did you see Christopher Abernathy's face?"

I shake my head.

"Were you aware that he has a black eye?"

"It's not—"

"What do you think the school's policy should be with regard to students who give other students black eyes?"

For a second I get why people hate Ms. Kenworthy. She's not letting me talk at all.

I say, "Yeah, but I don't think you know what was going on before that. I bet no one told you that Chris called Nelson brain damaged."

I can tell from her expression, no one did tell her that. But then she says, "That doesn't excuse—"

"Or that Chris was getting kids to sign a petition to have retards exterminated."

She goes quiet for a moment. Then she says, "Do you have a copy of this petition?"

I say, "No," wondering why she would ask me that. Then I get it: because she thinks I'm lying.

"I am not lying," I tell her. "You can ask any of the kids who were there. If they're not Chris's friends, they'll tell you that's exactly what happened."

Ms. Kenworthy picks up her pen like she wants to write something down. But instead, she holds it out in front of her like a sword. *Pass not, Anna Morris!* "Even if this is true, I'm not sure it changes my view that Nelson deserved suspension."

Yeah, right, I think, *because then you'd have to admit that you were wrong.*

This is so unfair. I will never think of Ms. Kenworthy as a decent person again.

Then she says, "But I will look into what you've told me."

Oh, great! Anna Morris, snitch extraordinaire.

Chris, Anna Morris tells me you were handing out a petition against retards, is this true?

Gosh, no, Ms. Kenworthy. I'll have to ask Anna why she would say such a thing.

I stand up. "You know what, just forget it."

Ms. Kenworthy looks startled. "I'm not going to forget it, Anna."

"Oh, right, you'll ask Chris, and he'll say, 'Uh, no.' And that'll be that."

"No, that will not be that." Ms. Kenworthy sounds frustrated.

Guess what, Ms. Kenworthy? I'm pretty frustrated too. You people pretend to be fair and wise. *Oh, trust us, we always do the right thing, look up to us, do what we say, we know best.* And then you pull something like this.

I think of Eve and Declan, of all the people who think you can't do anything because, ultimately, no one cares.

They were right.

I hate that they were right.

I don't want anyone to see me, so I run upstairs to the bathroom and lock myself in a stall. For a moment I push my hands hard against my eyes until I'm s... I'm not going to cry. When I take my hands away they're a little wet but not too bad.

Sniff once, twice . . .

Deep breath.

Okay, I'm not going to totally lose it.

I have to think of something else. I pick up my book bag and pull out the first book I find: Declan's book on disasters. As I open it, a piece of paper falls out.

It has Declan's handwriting on it. And it is not homework.

You don't write homework "For Her."

I shouldn't look at this. I should put it back inside the book and decide I never saw it.

But I don't care about shouldn'ts anymore, so I snatch it up, read:

For Her
You do not even look at me
With your blue eyes
You hide from everyone
Hope they never see you
But I can look at you
And hope you see me.

There should be a rule: All love poems should be addressed to someone. Like letters. *Dear So-and-So, I love you.*

Also, if you're going to compliment someone on

their blue eyes, you should make sure the person you're dating has blue eyes.

Or that she never sees this poem.

Numb, I think, *This is why he didn't want to make a big deal about being a couple at school. Because he's into someone else, someone he thinks he can't have.* I was right all along. Declan didn't pick me. I'm just second best.

Frantic, I think about the cards. The cards said we would be together, this wasn't just something I made up. But the cards also said there was an impostor. Is this what they meant? Is Declan the impostor? Or am I, for thinking I could be his girlfriend?

Then what about that final card, the Lovers? That was supposed to be me and Declan. He was my final card.

Only, clearly, I'm not his.

I check my watch, see that I'm going to be late to first period if I don't move. I stuff the poem back in the book, then the book back into my bag. Then I rush out into the hall . . .

And straight into Eve. Who grumbles, "Hey, thanks for the phone call."

I'm confused. What phone call? What is she talking about? Then I remember, I was supposed to call her after my "big date." I was so busy thinking about Nelson and Ms. Kenworthy all weekend, I forgot.

For a moment I'm tempted to show her the poem and tell her everything that happened at Declan's house. But I know exactly what she'll say. She'll say that Declan's a jerk and that I have to dump him right away. And if I don't agree, she'll think I'm a pathetic wuss.

It's always easy to say what should be done when you're not the one who has to do it.

Walking fast, I say, "Sorry. Things got . . . crazy."

"Oh, really?"

"Yeah . . . homework and stuff with my mom." I am walking, but Eve is following. She's not going to let this go. But she's going to have to because I can't talk about Declan right now.

"What's wrong?" she asks. "Did something happen?"

"Nothing happened." She wants something to have happened, I realize. Something awful, so she can feel sorry for me and be mad at Declan. Eve's one of those people, she always wants to think the worst of everyone. . . .

"So, what'd you guys do?" she asks.

I try to think of something to give her. "Watched TV. Talked."

I start up the stairs, but Eve stops. "Why are you being like this?"

I turn. "Like what? I'm not being anything."

"Yeah, come on, I've known you forever. You're freezing me out."

"Freezing you—?" Yeah, Eve, God forbid I don't tell you everything. God forbid you're not allowed to tell me what I can and can't do. "Why? 'Cause I won't tell you every little detail of my life?"

Eve's eyes go wide, she lifts her hands in the air. "I am not asking for every little detail—"

"Yes, you are. You're all like, 'What did you say? What did he say? What'd you do? What was it like?'" I feel my voice rising. "Just leave me alone about it, okay?"

"Leave you—?" Eve shakes her head. "Okay, first I'm not even good enough to have lunch with you and Declan. Then I'm not good enough to hear about your precious *date* with Declan. What next? I won't even be allowed to talk to you?"

Exasperated, I say, "No, of—"

But Eve just keeps going. "Fine. I won't talk to you. Only just one thing before I cease to darken your life."

She walks to the stairwell, then turns around. "I wasn't going to tell you this. Because we were friends and I thought it would hurt your feelings. But you know what? Now I don't care. So here's the scoop. Your so-called boyfriend was with another girl last week, and he looked pretty happy. And *that's* why I asked about your stupid date. Because I thought maybe he had broken up with you, and I thought you might need a friend."

Eve throws up her hands. "But I was so wrong, I see that now. You don't need a friend, you don't need anybody. You've got *Declan*. The only question is, who does Declan have?"

Then she storms up the stairs.

I can't believe it. Eve knows that there is a Her. She knows who Her is.

Which means . . . there is a Her.

Is she the girl walking next to me in the hallway?

The girl I see in the bathroom?

Or . . . anybody. It could be anybody.

In biology, I try to narrow down the list of suspects. On Zoe's World, people voted Elissa, Alexa, Jackie Gonzalez, and Chloe Deutscher as the girls most likely to date Declan. Elissa just started dating a sophomore, so I don't think it's her. Jackie's got a boyfriend at another school. Plus, she's really nice; I don't think she'd date someone else's guy. And Chloe's home sick with mono, so she can't be the girl Eve saw talking to Declan.

Then there's Alexa.

I look where she's sitting with Marnie. When Declan dumped her, everyone who had ever hated her felt like they could be catty about her—and it turned out a lot of people hated her. She hasn't been her diva self since she shoved me in the cafeteria. In fact, she's been acting very much like someone who does *not* want to be noticed.

But today she's grinning and cracking little jokes with Marnie. Why is she suddenly in such a good mood?

Alexa's eyes are blue. I'd forgotten that.

Mr. Fegelson starts drawing pictures of flowers on the white board as he talks about crossbreeding. As he asks us, "You ever wonder how daisies make other daisies? Why they don't get together with a rose instead, make a rose daisy?" Alexa whispers something to Marnie, looks over at me.

I want to ask, *What is your problem?*

You are. You stole my boyfriend. But guess what? I've stolen him back.

Mr. Fegelson asks, "Can anyone think of other strange pairings?"

I call out, "Sharks and porpoises."

Jack Montgomery says, "Sharks eat porpoises," and everyone laughs.

"Actually, not most sharks," says Mr. Fegelson. "But that's right, Anna. Sharks don't mate with porpoises for the same reason lions don't mate with lambs: They're genetically predisposed to mate with their own kind."

I say, "What about dogs? I mean, Dobermans can mate with . . . dachshunds, can't they?"

Mr. Fegelson smiles. "I'm not sure Dobies and dachsies could work on the level of sheer physics, but with dogs, you're talking about difference of breed, not difference of species."

"That's how you get mutts," says Alexa, wrinkling her nose.

"Mutts are the smartest dogs," I tell her.

"They're certainly the ugliest," says Alexa, and gives me a long, hard stare.

Mr. Fegelson says hastily, "I'm personally a big fan of mutts, but maybe we could get back to plant life?"

I can feel Alexa glaring at me. She scored, and she knows it. For a truly awful moment I feel like I'm going to burst into tears. I take a deep breath, rub the heel of my hand against my eyes.

Declan picked me. He could have gone out with any girl in school, and he picked me. The cards said he would and he did.

I hear Alexa whispering, hear Marnie giggle.

Then I remember: The cards said other things, too. Like . . . *impostor.*

Like . . . *powerlessness in the face of stronger forces.*

Like . . . *misery.*

I have never cut class. In chorus it's our last week to rehearse for our holiday concert, and I really should be there. Mr. Courtney is taking the holiday caroling very seriously this year; he wants to show everyone how good our choir can be.

But there's no way I can be in the same room with Declan right now. If I see him, I feel like I'll blurt out: *What's with this poem? Who's this girl you were talking to? Do you even like me anymore? Did you ever like me?*

So instead of going to chorus, I hide in the bathroom and try to think. Everything that's happened is spinning around in my head; I can't see any of it clearly or say, *Okay,* this *I know for sure.*

I try telling myself there are things I do know. Like . . . Declan likes someone else. The poem proves it.

But he could have written that poem a long time ago. He said he hadn't looked at the book for forever. It could even have been for Alexa—but then he found out she was evil and dumped her.

Yeah, right. And that's why she's looking so happy lately.

Or maybe Alexa's just trying to make me feel insecure, because that's what P&Ps do.

But then what about the girl Eve saw talking to Declan?

Perhaps Eve saw what she wanted to see. She's always doing that. Even with the cards, she was the one who said, *Oh, it means this.* But she doesn't actually know. She just acts like the big authority on everything.

God, I don't know what to believe. I have to talk to someone about this, someone who's not all tangled up in it already, who can say, *Yes, you're right to think this, but totally wrong about that.*

Most importantly, I need someone who won't spread it all over school.

I go to a pay phone and call Syd.

When it's just the two of us without Eve, Syd and I like to go to Central Park. Despite all the people, there's something private and quiet about the park. As I hurry down the street, I think, *In a little while I am going to feel much, much better. Syd is going to tell me I'm crazy, or she'll tell me what to do, or . . .*

Or whatever. I just know I'm going to feel better once I talk to Syd.

When I see her, I want to throw my arms around her,

say, *My savior!* But Syd is standing back a little, obviously not wanting to be hugged, so I just say, "Hey!"

"Hey."

There's a little pause. Then I say, "So, where do you want to go?"

"Wherever," says Syd.

As we walk, I ask Syd all kinds of questions: What's she been doing, how's Beesley, did she ever call that guy who has Tatiana?

When she answers "No" to that last question, I say, "Well, maybe we could call this weekend."

She nods like, *We'll see.* Then she says, "So, what's up? I feel like I haven't talked to you in forever."

I wrestle with how to start: *Poem? No. Declan? No. Alexa? No.* . . . Then I blurt out, "Eve is driving me crazy."

Syd looks down. The path is slippery with wet leaves, so we have to be careful. "How so?"

"This whole thing with Declan—she's acting bizarre, and I don't get it."

Syd looks surprised. "What do you mean?"

"Oh, like . . ." I think of Eve yelling, *Who does Declan have?* It hurts, and I start talking fast to get past it. "I feel like she's jealous, so she's trying to make me insecure. Today she told me she saw Declan talking to another girl and that he looked all happy."

Syd nods carefully. "But she said it in a nasty way, not like a friend."

Syd is quiet for a long time. I'm terrified she's going to say, *You sad, deluded girl. Your boyfriend's hot for someone else, everyone knows it, and you're pissed at your friend for telling you the truth?*

Then she says, "That's not cool. But I guess Eve's a little mad."

"About *what*? What have I done to Eve that's so horrible?"

Syd bites her lip.

"Has Eve been talking about me behind my back?"

"No . . ." Syd looks miserable. "Except I know she's upset that you haven't been around very much."

I want to scream. But if I do, Syd will back way off. So I take a deep breath and say, "I know I haven't got the whole boyfriend versus friends thing figured out yet."

Syd frowns. "You don't have to figure us out."

Exasperated, I sigh. "Okay, I won't."

There's a turn in the path coming. At one point it's not clear: Should Syd go first? Should I? She stops, lets me go first. Which is either *I'm sorry* or *I'm sick of you*, I'm not sure which.

Taking a deep breath, I say, "Look, I know I've been jerky lately, and I'm sorry. But things are kind of intense with Declan, and I don't know what to do."

Syd nods; we're almost back to being friends.

Then she says, "I think you should talk to him. That way, you'll know."

"Know what?"

"That you don't have to worry."

"I'm not worried," I tell her. "I'm annoyed because sometimes I think . . ."—*that Declan wants to be with someone else*—"that some people think Declan should be with someone else."

Syd shakes her head. "Why do you *care* what they think?"

That is one of my least favorite questions of all time. The fact is, everyone cares what other people think. But people—well, certain people—act all superior and say, *Well, why do you care?* Even if they secretly care just as much.

I try to explain. "Syd, if you had a boyfriend, wouldn't you hate it if everyone said, 'Oh, he should be going out with . . . like, Eve'?"

"I wouldn't care," she says steadily, "as long as I knew he really liked me and not Eve."

"I *know* that," I say carefully to cover up how mad I am. "I know that. Just . . ."

"Just what?"

"I need advice about what to do." Syd looks puzzled, so I try to explain. "A little part of me is worried that he still likes Alexa, the girl he used to go out with."

Before I can add, *Or some other girl,* Syd asks, "How come?"

I can't tell her about the poem, I can't. "No specific reason. And, actually, I know he doesn't still like her, but . . ." Even as I'm talking, I know I should stop, that I'm not making sense because I'm not telling the whole truth. But I can't. I can't tell Syd the whole truth because I know what she'll say, and I can't hear that.

Syd says flat out, "If someone's making you this crazy, he's not treating you right."

Okay, great, Syd, but it's not that simple. "It's not Declan who's making me crazy."

"Then who is it?"

I throw up my hands. Why can Syd not get that the issue here is Eve trying to make me jealous? "I don't know. This girl, Alexa. Eve, a little bit, to be honest—"

Syd stops dead in her tracks. Her hands are bunched into fists. "Okay, just stop. Now it's Eve's fault? You have got to be kidding me. Anna, what's happened to you? All this blah-blah about Declan. Who cares, Anna? Seriously. Who. Cares."

I flinch. I have never seen Syd this angry.

She folds her arms, says, "You used to be the

coolest person I knew; now you're totally boring. 'What should I do? What should I do?'" It takes me a moment to get that she's imitating me. "You're asking the cards, you're asking Eve, you're asking me. I mean, if you really want my opinion, I say dump the creep. He sounds like a loser."

Then she takes a step toward me, asks, "But what do *you* think, Anna? Or *do* you even think anymore?"

I am thinking. A mile a minute. I'm thinking, *Declan is not a loser, he's nice.* I'm thinking, *Just because I haven't been around doesn't give Eve the right to say what she said to me.* I'm thinking, *What did I do to make you this angry at me? And why didn't I figure this out? How did I get things so wrong?*

But I never get to ask Syd any of that because she's walking away. And somehow that feels right. If I were Syd, I'd walk away from me. She's headed home, but I can't follow. I'm scared of her. I'm scared of everybody.

I turn around and start walking in the other direction. I'm not really sure where I'm going, just that I need to be away. At one point I walk too close to a tree and a branch whips across my face. It doesn't really hurt, but I still feel like crying.

This is somebody's fault. It has to be. It feels too bad not to be.

I think of how this started, with the cards, the stupid cards. Eve saying we should do a reading. I think: *This is Eve's fault.*

But I listened to her. So, really, it's my fault.

It's Declan's fault. For lying to me. But then why didn't the cards warn me? Why did they promise I would be happy? Did I do something wrong that messed it all up? If I did, somebody please tell me what I can do to make it right.

My dad lives on the other side of the park, and when I come out onto the street, I head to his place without thinking. He probably won't be home, but I have the key. As I walk, I think, *I'll call Mom from there, tell her I'll be home later. Or maybe not at all, I don't know.*

As I put the key in the lock, I hear a voice from inside the apartment. A man's voice. I open the door to see my dad on the phone. He looks up as I come in, says quickly, "Wait, she's here. Yeah . . . it's okay, she's . . . I'll call you back."

He drops the phone, pulls me into his arms. "Oh, my God, where were you?"

Why is he so freaked? I look past my dad, see Russell sitting on the couch. Russell shouldn't be here. And why does he look like he's been crying?

I say, "What happened?"

My dad gives a strange laugh, rubs his forehead. "Uh, yeah. What did happen? I got a call from Russell, saying he was at school, but he couldn't find you."

"No . . ." I shake my head. "Russell has judo today."

My dad glances back at Russell, who yells, "No, I don't. Judo's Tuesday and Friday."

There's something wrong with what he's saying. There has to be. I did not leave Russell alone at school. I would never, ever do that. "Yeah, but today's . . ."

My dad frowns. "Today's Monday, Anna."

"Right, but . . ." There is a way this works out, a way I am right, I know there is.

My dad stares at me. "Where have you been all this time?"

"I was . . ." *Talking to my friend. Who's not my friend anymore. Because she hates me, because I'm . . . awful and . . .*

I left him. I left Russell all alone.

What if he hadn't called Dad? What if he'd tried to go home by himself?

"Anna? What were you thinking?"

"I don't know!" I burst into tears. "I don't know what I thought. But I'm sorry, okay? I'm sorry!"

And before my dad can ask if I know what could have happened to a seven-year-old alone in New York City, I run into the other room and slam the door.

TWELVE

THE QUEEN OF WANDS

Kind, interested in others, devoted

You can't cry forever. Eventually, you run out of tears and your head starts to hurt. But for a long time I just lie on my dad's bed with my face pressed into the pillow. From the other room, I hear voices. My dad talking to my mom, asking Russell what he'd like for dinner, the clatter of pots and pans. Life going on. Without me.

Then a knock at the door.

I sit up, feel very strange. From the time on the clock, it's only been two hours. But I feel like I slept the whole day and night through. Not sure of my voice, I croak, "Yeah?"

My dad opens the door. I hear the *ping kapow* of a

video game. Special treat for Russell. Dad says, "Feeling like visitors?"

"Uh, sure." My dad comes in and sits down on the edge of the bed. I tuck myself up, wrap my arms around my knees. For a moment we just sit there. Then I say, "I am *so* sorry."

"I know you are, baby. I know you are." He reaches out, pushes some damp hair out of my face. "What's going on? You don't seem very happy these days."

"I'm okay."

"Not what your mom says. Not what I'm seeing."

I trace the pattern of my dad's quilt. "I don't know. I don't feel like I know anything anymore."

"You? You're the smartest girl I know."

I look up. "No, I'm not, Dad. Not always, you know?" My voice breaks. Guess tears replenish themselves pretty quick.

My dad wraps me up in his arms, puts his hand on my head so I can stay down and not look at anything. He keeps saying "Okay" over and over.

Then he says, "I think maybe we've been asking a little too much of you, your mom and me."

I sit up. "No, Dad, I don't mind taking care of Russell, really."

"I know you don't. But everybody needs a break. A chance to sit back and say, 'You know what? The world has to turn without me today.'" For some reason, that makes me laugh. "Yeah, you look like a girl who's had the world on her shoulders lately."

"I feel like I keep trying to do things right, and somehow I end up making stuff worse."

"I doubt that," says my dad.

From the other room, Russell yells, "Dad!"

My dad gets up, opens the door. "I'm talking with Anna now, Russell. Okay?" He shuts the door, comes back.

I say, "Remember what you said about fate, that other people were a big factor in what happened to us?"

My dad nods. "Key in the mix, yeah. We were talking about guys, if I remember."

"Well, I feel like I want to do what other people want me to, what they expect, you know? But it's like the rules keep changing."

My dad demands, "Whose rules?" I don't know how to answer that. "Okay, let me get something clear here. Is the right thing always what other people want? Is that the voice of destiny? If other people say it must be, it must be?"

I think about this. "No, obviously. But we have to listen to other people. I hate when people say, 'Oh, who cares? I'm just going to do what I want.'"

"I know you do, and it's one of the best things about you. But where's Anna in all this? You seem like a girl who could create her own destiny. What do *you* want?"

I falter. "What I want involves other people. . . ."

My dad says, "Oh," very slowly. Then: "Well, I guess that's true for most of what we want in life. I don't know what to tell you there, sweetie. If other people don't want what you want . . . well, you just have to find someone who does. There'll be someone, I promise you. A lot of someones."

I say, "Yeah, yeah," because I know this is just my dad making me feel better—even though it does make me feel better. "So, what do you do in the meantime?"

"What you can," says my dad.

After dinner my dad drives us back to my mom's. Russell falls asleep in the back. As we roll through the park, I look out the window, watching the cars and thinking that any one of them could have hit Russell today.

Not doing what you can can lead to seriously bad things. I knew it before, but I really get it now.

But as we come out of the park, I think it's also true that you can't do everything. Like, there's nothing I can do to make Declan like me if he likes Miss Blue Eyes. No matter what the cards say.

Maybe the universe doesn't have anything planned for us. Maybe the cards are a total lie, a way to make you feel you know what's coming and you can plan for it, even make it happen. Like in croquet, when you see one ball close to the wicket, and you know if you hit your ball just so, you can knock it through. That's what I've been trying to do. Nudge everything where I thought it needed to go, even if it kept hitting the wicket.

When we get home, my mom gives me a long kiss on top of the head and says, "Tomorrow we're going to talk about some changes, okay?"

I'm so glad to be home and have everything be okay that I don't want anything to change, but I say, "Okay," then head off to my room.

As I come in, I hear a rumbling purr and see Mouli creep out from under my desk. Normally, I would crouch down, try to get him to come to me. But it's never worked, and tonight I'm too tired.

Opening the door, I say, "You know what, Mouli? If you want to go over to Russell's, that's cool. You want to stay here, that's cool too." And I flop down on my bed because I have never been so exhausted.

Then I feel something small and heavy on my stomach. I look up, see a fat orange paw, then a fat orange face. Slowly, because I don't want to scare him,

I draw my hand along his back. Mouli collapses at my side, purrs.

For a while we just sit there. Then, gently, so as not to disturb him, I stand up and get my notebook. Turning to a fresh page, I start writing.

I'm a little late to school the next day. By the time I get there, the halls are packed. Some kids are running to class, others are frantically trying to finish their homework. There are lots of little groups. As I put my coat away, I see Katy Marx laughing nervously over something Elissa has said, because she wants Elissa to like her. Chris Abernathy shouting like an idiot, just to let everyone know he's here; Kyle echoing him, because who's Kyle without Chris? Sheila Davis patting on lip gloss, wiping it off, patting it on again, looking around to see if anyone noticed. Everybody so worried about doing what's cool or acceptable. Nobody wanting to be punished by the great gods or offend them in any way.

Unzipping my bag, I take out my notebook, snap the rings open, and remove what I was working on last night. It took me a few tries to get it right, but I think it's just about there.

I go to the community bulletin board, where they post all the school news and events. Stuff like the

Spring Fling and sign-up sheets for school plays or team tryouts. Now there's a little article on Alexa getting a part in a new commercial, a reminder about the holiday party on Friday, tryouts for the boys' soccer team. I move some things around, create a big blank space. Then I take a thumbtack and stick my piece of paper right in the center.

FREE NELSON KOBLINER!

Sign here to end Nelson's suspension.

If you were in the lunchroom on Wednesday, December 9th, then you know what really happened. If you know what really happened, then you know that it's wrong that Nelson was suspended while certain other people were not punished at all.

Tell Ms. Kenworthy she was wrong.

Ask her to look at injustice in her own school.

FREE NELSON KOBLINER!

Behind me I hear, "Interesting."

I turn, see Eve. For a moment we don't say anything.

Then she reaches over and puts her name on the petition.

The hallway starts emptying out. We're going to be

late to class, but that doesn't matter. I blurt out, "I'm sorry . . ." just as Eve says, "Yeah, so . . ."

Then she says, "You go."

I smile. "No, you can go."

Her eyes narrow. "You totally owe me an apology."

"You owe me one."

Eve waves her hands. "Okay, okay, okay. Let's do Truth."

Truth is one of our sleepover games. Late at night, right before we go to sleep, each person has to tell a deeply embarrassing thing about herself and the other two must be okay with it. It's our way of making sure there's nothing important we don't know about one another. Also, it's fun to see who can come up with the most shocking thing. As you might guess, Eve usually wins there, but I think she lies sometimes.

Eve surprises me by saying, "I'll go first." Then, folding her arms like she's defending herself against her own words, she says, "Truth: I know people think you could do a lot better than me for a best friend."

This is so not what I expected that it takes me a moment to understand. Then I remember that crack on Zoe's World. How she said I should stop hanging with GoofyGothGrl. How Elissa pretended I was eating alone when I was eating with Eve. . . .

I say, "Truth: They're wrong."

Eve leans against the wall. "Truth: You could do the whole P&P thing if you wanted. I can't. So when you weren't around, I thought, 'Oh, it's dump the freak time.'"

I take this in for a moment. "Truth: I knew you thought that, and it pissed me off. How could you think I would be that low?"

"Because people are."

"But I'm *not*. Back to Truth. I was really mad at you for saying what you did about Declan and that girl." Eve nods apologetically. "But later I realized you didn't say it just to be cruel."

Eve looks skeptical. "Are you sure? I was feeling pretty cruel."

"Yeah, I got that. But here's how I know you were right to tell me, and here's why I've been so nuts lately." I reach into my bag, take out Declan's poem. Handing it to Eve, I say, "Truth: Declan wrote this. Please note I do not have blue eyes."

As Eve reads, I can tell from her expression, she's genuinely shocked. "That—" Then she stops herself. "It could be nothing, you know. Like a really, really bad song lyric."

Eve is saying this for one reason: She is my friend. If I want this to be nothing, she will say—at least to my face—that it's nothing. At that moment I can't believe I ever did or said anything to hurt our friend-ship. I hope we're friends until we're as old as Mrs. Rosemont.

Eve will forget she ever saw this, if that's what I want. And if I want to tear Declan's head off, she will hold him down while I do it.

That is true friendship.

That afternoon I stay in the practice room after class to apologize to Mr. Courtney for missing chorus. He's sitting at the piano like always. As I approach him, he says without looking up, "Miss Anna Morris. Where were you yesterday?"

Uh, well, Mr. Courtney, I was hiding in the bathroom because I couldn't deal with seeing my boyfriend, who probably isn't my boyfriend anymore. Before I can come up with some lame excuse, he waves his hand. "Yeah, yeah, I know. You didn't feel great or you had to work on your English paper or whatever. Well, don't skip out on me again. We're three days away from the greatest caroling this school's ever seen, and my chorus needs you."

I say, "Right. Because the altos would just die with-out me."

"Well, they wouldn't die, I wouldn't let them die." Mr. Courtney says "die" like it has two syllables:

"die-eh." "But the chorus wouldn't be as excellent and sublime as I can make it, and that I will not tolerate."

Somehow the words "excellent" and "sublime" don't go with my vision of myself as a singer. If the chorus didn't have Lara or Bridget, you'd know it. Me—there's just one less squeak. And I guess I'm in the mood for honesty, because I say, "That's nice, but let's face it, it's not like I'm some great singer."

Courtney's head snaps up. "Who says?"

"I do."

"Wrong." Mr. Courtney pounds on the piano keys. "Wrong, wrong, wrong. I say who's a great singer and who is not a great singer."

Intrigued, I ask, "So . . . which am I?"

"You are not that great a singer," he says flatly. "But you are a superb member of the chorus. You work hard, you memorize your part. You follow your chorus instructor"—bang, bang on the piano—"and you are kind, helpful, and supportive of your fellow chorus members. In fact, Anna? You may be the best singer this chorus has ever had. So you better be at practice all week and singing on Friday."

I don't know if I believe what Courtney's saying about me being the best singer this chorus has ever had, but from the look on his face, I know he believes it. And for the first time since the Declan mess started, I feel like one morning I might wake up and the first thing I think won't be, *I am such an idiot.*

"Okay. Thanks, Mr. Courtney."

"For what?" he says disdainfully.

"Um, I don't know, but thanks."

I head to the door, then I hear, "Hey, Anna," and turn around. "There are so many people wandering around, thinking it's all about them—but you know what? They're not so much. They're running around going 'I'm somebody,' but they don't have any time to do anything worthwhile. So busy being special, they don't bother being any *good.* People like that bore me to death." He plays a little something. "Now get out of here."

As I head upstairs to meet Eve by the lockers, I wonder if she managed to get hold of Syd. The plan is for us all to get together this afternoon at my house. I figure if Eve tells Syd I am finally sane again, she will agree to hang. Then I'll make it up to her by calling Tat's new owner.

And then everything will be back to normal.

Except . . .

Except I may have to break up with Declan.

I will definitely get points for dumping the hottest guy at school. But if Declan starts going out with someone else right away, everyone will know it was a preemptive dump, so not as impressive.

But if he likes someone else, I should dump him. If I try to dump him and he says no, then I'll know he really likes me. But what if he's so hurt that I tried to dump him that he doesn't say anything, but he still really likes me . . . ?

I want to stop thinking about this. Now.

Eve is sitting on the floor next to her locker, which is open. She is surrounded by junk. Magazines, CDs, clothes, candy wrappers, even last year's math book. I say, "What are you doing?"

She crumples up an old potato chip bag. "With winter break coming, I thought I'd clean out my locker. I don't know, though. Now I'm not so into it."

So she starts shoving the mess back into the locker. "Oh, hey, got Syd. She says yes for after school. I had to reassure her you were no longer insane."

"As opposed to you," I say, snatching a sweater off the floor and folding it.

"As opposed to me," Eve agrees, giving the chaos a last push. "And she's bringing Beesley, like you asked."

She closes the door to her locker. And that's when I see my locker. To be more specific, I see the rose. Taped to the door of my locker.

It's not the boring, normal red rose you see in cheesy movies and greeting cards. This one's so dark red, it's almost black, with flares of scarlet at the edges. It may be the coolest thing I've ever seen.

Carefully, so as to not rip the stem, I pull the tape free of the door. Then I get out my Swiss Army key chain and snip the tape from the stem. I twirl the rose between my thumb and forefinger. Smell it. It has a deep, real rose smell.

"Whoa." Eve comes up behind me. "Did it come with anything? Like a note?"

I look. "Don't see one."

"But it has to be Declan, right? Who else would assume you'd know who it was from?"

That makes sense. I smell the rose again.

Agitated, Eve says, "So what do you think? Is this an 'I'm sorry' rose? An 'I'm seriously into you' rose? What?"

I think. Maybe Declan saw the Free Nelson petition and this is his way of saying it's okay? Maybe he gets that he was a jerk the other day and wants to apologize?

Or maybe, just maybe, he remembered that he left that stupid poem in the book and he's worried what I'll think. If so, this is not a terrible way to make up for it.

I go into the bathroom, wet a paper towel, and wrap it around the stem.

Eve says, "You have to wear it tomorrow. Put it in

your hair or something." I shake my head. "At least show the guy you got it."

I hesitate. I can see what Eve is thinking. But somehow the rose is something more than that. It's not a thing to be shown around and used. It's something to be kept secret and safe. I put it inside my coat to protect it on the way home.

I don't know what I'm worried about more: that Mouli will turn psycho and attack Beesley or that Syd will attack me. Syd, apparently, is worried about the same thing. When Syd arrives at my house holding Beesley, I can't tell who's more nervous—her or Beese.

She glances at Mouli, who's bristling on the floor. "Is this okay?"

I pick Mouli up, stroke his fur. "It's your old pal," I tell him. "Beesley. Be nice." Mouli's eyes narrow, but he stops bristling. Beese shrinks into Syd, tries to climb higher on her shoulder. She whispers something in his ear, then sets him down. After a moment I set Mouli down.

We watch the two of them pace around at our feet for a moment.

"Someone's missing," I say.

"Yeah," says Syd.

And we go call Tat's new owner.

Later, as we're sitting on my floor trying to keep Mouli and Beesley away from some Chinese food we found in the fridge, Eve says, "It's time to talk about Declan."

Immediately, Syd and I say, "No."

Eve says to me, "You have to tell her."

Sighing, I get the poem out of my bag, hand it to Syd. "From Declan," explains Eve.

"And not to me," I add.

Syd reads. At first she doesn't say anything, just sets it down on the floor like she can't stand to look at it. Then she says softly, "Man, people are mean. And stupid."

Eve says, "Hold on, we don't know that this means what we think it means."

"Well, let me ask you this," I say, taking the poem off the floor before Mouli shreds it. "Did the girl you saw talking to Declan have blue eyes?"

Eve concentrates on getting a dumpling out of the carton. "I've decided I was wrong about that. So you should just forget about it."

"Oh, come on. You said it—you can't expect me not to care. At least tell me who it was."

"Nope. I was wrong, so I'm not going to. Besides," she tells Syd, "we didn't tell you about the rose yet."

Syd perks up. "Rose?"

"Declan left one on her locker."

Syd shakes her head. "Does he seem like the kind of guy who dates two girls at the same time?"

I think. "Maybe I'm dumb, but I really don't think so. Besides, if he was? No way Zoe's World wouldn't be all over it."

"Exactly," says Eve, who it seems is now Declan's biggest champion. "So I say we forget about the poem, forget the other girl, and trust in the cards."

Laughing, I say, "Okay," and ask Syd to pass me the fortune cookies.

Mine says: *Life is like a storm. Venture forth, but bring an umbrella.*

THIRTEEN

THE LOVERS

First love, romance, connection

The week before winter break is always totally crazy. There are, of course, finals, and everyone competing to see who can be the most stressed out, the most sleep deprived, the most *absolutely insane*. This year I might win that one; this Oedipus essay is making me nuts. I have two days to go, and I still haven't gotten any further than, *Was Oedipus responsible for his fate?* Not that Ms. Taramini is any help. When I told her I couldn't decide yes or no, she said either answer was right, as long as I backed it up. Gee, thanks.

But people are doing a lot of stuff besides finals. There are the Collectors, kids who collect for UNICEF, donate coats and winter boots, or do penny drives for world hunger. There are the Cooks, who are busy planning what dessert to make for the holiday party. There are the Crabs, who go around saying it's all a stupid waste of time, so who cares?

And this year there's the Carolers, Mr. Courtney's chorus, who, on the last day before break, go around caroling throughout the school. We even get out of class that day, because everyone knows you don't do anything except eat candy and pass out presents. We will go from floor to floor, singing in every classroom. Then we'll finish up in the library, singing three songs to kick off the holiday party.

Mr. Courtney is in a total fever. He says that last year he was too busy "molding" the chorus to accomplish anything serious. So this is our first big public appearance, and he wants to show everyone what "my chorus" can do. Not only do we rehearse during class, but for the last few days we are actually let out of fifth period as well to rehearse. For me, this means no gym, so I'm thrilled. These rehearsals are dead serious. No note passing, no whispering, no giggling. Not unless you want an eraser thrown at you.

By now we're all so sick of these songs, it's hard to sing them with any enthusiasm. Standing next to me on Wednesday, Bridget rubs her nose with her sweater sleeve and says, "I *hate* 'O Tannenbaum!'"

I say, "I'll *puke* a jingle bell if I have to sing about them one more time."

Then Declan comes in. We're back to talking almost every night. I never said anything about the rose on the phone last night—or about the poem, for that matter. Eve's right. One cancels the other out.

Besides, all week, he's made a little stop as he comes into chorus. No big thing, just a "Hey, how you doing?" Mostly to me, but to the other altos, too. Which is nice, because I once told him everyone thinks the sopranos are the chorus hotties, and this must be his way of saying we're cute too.

Today as he stops, I say, "Bridget and I are trying to figure out which song we hate most."

"Oh, uh . . ." He looks down at the floor—probably because Mr. Courtney is watching. "All of them kind of give me the heebies at this point."

Bridget gets left out of conversations unless you include her, so I say to her, "That sounds about right."

Bridget is also looking down. She says shyly, "Yeah."

Declan nods, puts his hands tighter in his pockets. "Yeah."

Then he says, "Well, see you after," and goes to sit down.

As Mr. Courtney starts warming us up with "A-a-a-a's," I think, *Wait a minute. Something just happened.*

I glance at Declan. He is staring straight out in front of him. But his face is red.

I look at Bridget. She is staring straight down at her music, even though we're supposed to be off book. Her face is pink.

Mr. Courtney calls, "Ms. Halsey, eyes up, please."

Blinking, Bridget looks up. Not completely.

But just enough for me to see her beautiful blue eyes.

That night I go home, sit down in front of my computer, and write my Oedipus essay.

The night before the holiday party, I set out all the things I'll need the next day. On my chair I put out my outfit. I want to wear my velvet pants, because they're green and I love them. On top of them I lay a red sweater. Sure, red and green is corny, but I don't care. I like it.

Next to the chair, I put my baked goods for the party. This year I tried to do gingerbread men. They came out a little . . . warped.

Next to them I put Declan's *Disaster!* book.

The next morning I get to school early. Ms. Taramini has graded our Oedipus papers, and as I won't be in class, I want to get it now and see my grade. I knock on the door, hear, "Come in."

As I open the door, Ms. Taramini smiles. "Hi, Anna. I have your paper right here." I look at her face for a clue: *You did great! By the way, I'm failing you.*

I see nothing—as usual. Taking my paper, I say, "Thanks. Have a great holiday."

She smiles. "You too."

I go out into the hall. Sitting on the radiator, I read:

WAS OEDIPUS RESPONSIBLE
FOR HIS FATE?
by Anna Morris

Did Oedipus have any choice, or was his whole life decided before he was even born? The gods said he would murder his father and marry his mother. But is there anything he could have done to stop it?

In my opinion, yes. For one thing, Oedipus could have never gotten married. That would have solved that problem. Or he could have married somebody younger and so been sure he wasn't marrying his mother. If he had thought a little bit about it, he could have avoided many of his problems, I think.

As for murdering his father, that's a little harder. In times of war, people often kill people they don't know anything about, so it might have been difficult to avoid that part of his fate.

Strangely, where Oedipus made his mistakes was in working so hard not to have the fate decreed for him. Everything he did to avoid his destiny led him to fulfill the prophecy. This is because there was so much he didn't know. He acted on a little piece of the truth, not knowing there were much bigger truths that would have affected his actions.

Where Oedipus went really wrong, I think, was in not believing the truth when the prophet Tiresias revealed it to him. Even though the gods had punished him with famine and people were starving, he said, "No, no, don't believe it, not happening, you're lying, shut up." No one can know everything, but if you refuse to listen when someone's trying to help you, then you are responsible for what happens.

So was Oedipus doomed by fate? Partly. He had responsibility for his own actions but not control over everything. This is why we feel sorry for him. Because no one has ultimate control. We can only try to do what's right and admit when we're wrong.

At the bottom of the page I see the grade Ms. Taramini wrote: *A*.

Because I had to work so hard on this paper, I was convinced I had messed it up. I can't believe I got an A. For the longest moment I just stare at it. Somehow it feels like I got more than the paper right. I still don't understand Ms. Taramini, but I don't think I hate her anymore.

Then I see the clock. I'm about to be late for chorus. I cut my way through the crowd and start running down the stairs. I'm going so fast that I run smack into someone.

"Hey," says Someone.

I say, "Sorry, major dork move, sorry."

Then I see who I've crashed into.

Nelson.

Who is suspended. And so not supposed to be in school.

Before I can say more than "Hey!" the crowd pushes forward, carrying Nelson upstairs and me down. I yell up, "See you at the party!" But I'm not sure he hears me.

By the time I get to chorus, everyone is already scrambling into place. Mr. Courtney is running up and down the line, adjusting the space in between people, lifting heads up, turning music folders the right way up. I scoot in behind Bridget just in time. Declan is all the way in the back with the basses, so I won't get to see him before . . .

But I don't have to think about that now.

Mr. Courtney claps his hands. "All right, people. I want an orderly procession. No giggling, no slovenliness. We are a *chorus*. We conduct ourselves as professionals." He glares at us, then takes off his glasses. "'Cause even if you don't get paid and I don't get paid much, when you're not goofing off and acting silly, you can sound . . . almost decent." He puts his glasses back on. "So let's go out there and show 'em that the Eberly Middle School Chorus is not a bunch of nerds, geeks, and losers, all right?"

We cheer and march out the door to "O Tannenbaum!"

As we go through the school, I admit, I'm worried that people will laugh, even throw things. And, sure, from their expressions, you can tell some people start off thinking it's lame. But the longer we sing, the more they get into it. By the second classroom, people are applauding as we leave. Individually, we might be nerds, geeks, and losers. But together we're great. For the very first time ever, it is cool to be in chorus.

I look at Mr. Courtney. When he first came here, everyone thought he was seriously strange. But he didn't care. And I guess he's taught the chorus not to care either.

In some ways, it doesn't matter if you have a great voice. What's neat is hearing all these voices at once, the separate parts all doing different things, then everything coming together. Everyone's weaknesses are covered by someone else's strength. And everyone's strengths help cover someone's weaknesses.

We go through all the administration offices, including Ms. Kenworthy's. When she sees me, she gives me a big smile. I'm so startled, I miss a whole bar and have to catch up. Why on earth is Ms. Kenworthy smiling at me? The last time she saw me, I told her she was a jerk.

Finally, we arrive in the library. As people come in for the party, we sing three songs to welcome them. Then, when everyone's here and the place is packed, we finish up with "Jingle Bells"—not the standard "Jingle Bells," but the joke lyrics about Batman. We sing it completely straight, in four-part harmony. Everyone starts cracking up. On the last verse Mr.

Courtney shouts, "Everybody!" and hundreds of people sing, ". . . broke his leg!" Then they start clapping and cheering. In the craziness Lara presents Mr. Courtney with a bouquet. He goes bright red. Sticking it under his arm, he starts applauding with everyone else.

As we start breaking formation, Declan says, "Wow, that was wild."

"Yeah," I say, watching everyone crowd the tables to get the best desserts. "Yeah, it really was."

Then I remember what I have to do. Nodding toward the stacks, I say, "Could we . . . ?"

Declan smiles. "You know what people will think."

"I don't mind."

We go deep into the nonfiction stacks. Reaching into my bag, I pull out *Disaster!* "I wanted to give this back."

Declan doesn't take the book. "You can hang on to it, I don't—"

"It has something in it that I think you want. Something I wasn't supposed to see."

Declan shakes his head like he doesn't know what I'm talking about.

"A poem?"

"Oh." He steps back, drops his head. "Oh, man, you weren't supposed to . . . Wow, this is embarrassing."

"Right. So." I hold out the book. After a moment Declan takes it.

"I wrote that last year," he says. "Not when we were—"

"Well, maybe you should give it to whomever you wrote it for." Declan looks at me. "She's here, right? I was just standing next to her?" Declan stares at me. "I think her name is . . . Bridget?"

Declan's mouth quirks. I say, "Bridget's the reason you joined chorus, isn't she?"

Declan sighs. "A little."

I was prepared for it to hurt when Declan finally admitted it. But it doesn't. All of a sudden, I feel like I can say anything. "So, why didn't you ask her out, you dumbbell?"

"She'd never go out with me."

I'm so shocked, I don't know what to say. Because Bridget's okay, but she's not by any means a hottie. Struggling to find a way to say this without insulting her, I say, "Wait a minute. You went out with Alexa, but you think you can't get Bridget? That doesn't make sense."

He shakes his head. "Guys don't think Alexa's so hot. Girls think she's hot. Like, if you could pick someone to look like, you'd probably pick her, right?"

I so want to say no. But I have to admit this is true, so I nod.

"Right, but to guys, she's this skinny, stuck-up chick who thinks she's all that. But she kind of isn't. I mean, you don't say no, but—"

I interrupt. "Why'd you go out with her, then? If she's such a loser?"

He shrugs. "Like I said, you don't say no."

"But then you bad-mouth her?"

"Come on, I didn't say anything bad about her till now."

Yeah, but you went out with her. You let her think you liked her. You got off on her liking you—but all the while you liked this other person. . . .

I can't tell—am I mad for Alexa, or am I mad for myself? Do Alexa and I have something in common? Weirdness alert!

I get back to the one thing I understand. "So you like Bridget."

He squirms. "Yeah."

I remember something. "That note you sent me, about Marnie's party. Was that for me or her?"

He goes red. "I meant it for her, but when you got it, that was okay too."

"But you meant it for Bridget! Why didn't you tell me to give it to her? Point or something?"

"I don't know! All of a sudden, you said yes, and I was like, 'God, I can't say, "Oh, sorry, that was for

someone else."' That would have been totally jerky."
He looks down at his shoes. "I didn't think someone
like you would ever go out with me. So when you said
yes, I thought, 'Why not?'"

"Like Alexa."

"No, totally not. That was a party thing. She
started kissing me, and all of a sudden, we were supposed to be in love or something. I never liked her. I
did . . ." He pushes at my hand with his finger. "I did
really like you. I thought you were cool. I mean, you
were one of the only people who was ever nice to me
before all . . . this."

"So, what? You thought we were meant to be?"

He smiles crookedly. "I don't know. Maybe?"

I'm about to tell him that figuring out the difference between what is and what's meant to be is a lot
harder than he thinks. That just because something
happens to you doesn't mean you should just go
along with it—even if it's what everyone else wants.

Instead, I point to the book in his hand. After a
moment I say, "So, will you ask Bridget out now,
please?"

He shakes his head. "That's so not cool to you."

"Hey, if I say it's cool, then it's cool. Come on."

Taking Declan's hand, I pull him across the library
to where Bridget is drinking punch. That's one of her

ways of hiding—putting something like a cup or a cookie in front of her face.

I say, "Declan wants to talk to you."

Her eyes widen above the cup. Suddenly, she coughs. I take the cup before she spills, set it aside.

Bridget stammers, "A-about what?"

I look over at Declan. He has gone completely red and won't take his eyes off the floor. For a split second I see Ark-Ark, the nerd he used to be—the nerd I guess he still is, in some ways—and I like him again. For a second I don't want to give him up.

But he wasn't ever this way with me, so I tell Bridget, "Declan has something for you."

She looks nervous. "Like what?"

I tap *Disaster!* Declan looks at me, panicked, shakes his head frantically.

I say, "It's hers, right? Then you should give it to her."

Reluctantly, Declan takes the poem out of the book, hands it to Bridget. As she reads it, she goes an even brighter pink. But I can tell from her blue eyes, she's really happy.

I start walking away. Bridget looks up, says, "Wait," and points to the air between me and Declan.

I grin. "Wasn't meant to be."

As I walk away, I see that Declan has his hands

deep in his jacket pockets. Bridget has crossed her arms in front of her chest. But after a few minutes Declan takes his hands out of his pockets and Bridget unfolds her arms. He says something, and she laughs.

I look around the room. Does anyone know that Anna and Declan are no more? That a new couple has arrived? Apparently not. Bridget wasn't on anyone's list to get Declan, so they can't see it, even though it's in front of them. Even Alexa, who's laughing with Marnie and Elissa. I guess she's over him—if she was ever really into him.

As I check out the dessert table to see if anyone has eaten my gingerbread guys, I realize I never asked Declan about the rose. But I guess that doesn't matter now.

I look for Eve and see her talking to Mr. Courtney—or rather, Mr. Courtney talking to her. He must be trying to get her to join chorus, because she makes a pleading face: *Rescue me!* Taking my plate of cookies as an excuse, I head over to them.

I'm almost there when I trip and the gingerbread men go flying. Crouching on the floor to pick them up, thinking how they've gone from weird to inedible, I see what I tripped over: a pair of sneakers sticking out from behind the checkout desk.

Nelson says, "God . . . sorry about my stupid feet."

I hold out the plate. "Crippled gingerbread men? The lint makes them extra special."

Nelson examines the plate. "I'll take one with no arms, please."

I hand him an armless one, saying, "I like the legless ones myself."

"The misshapen head ones are good."

"I worked especially hard on those."

"Shows."

I sit down cross-legged on the floor, put the cookies in between us. "So, is this part of your punishment, making you come to the holiday party?"

Nelson smiles. "Nah, they let me come back a few days ago. It's a weird deal when Ms. Kenworthy calls your house, man. Particularly if it's to apologize. My mom was like, 'Wait, are you talking about my kid?'"

"Ms. Kenworthy *apologized*?"

"Yeah." Nelson picks through the cookies. "I figured you knew 'cause . . . well, anyway. You weren't in gym, so."

It takes me a second to decipher this. It means: *I thought you knew because Ms. Kenworthy said you were the reason she revoked the suspension. I would have said thank you, but you weren't in gym this week, so I didn't see you.*

I say, "That's okay. I'm just really glad."

Then Nelson says, "I, uh . . ." just as I say, "So, what . . ."

He points. "You go first."

"I was just going to ask how the graphic novel was going."

Nelson looks surprised. I guess no one ever asks him about his novel. "Good. I had a lot of time to work on it."

"You must be pretty close to done."

He shakes his head. "Nah, like . . . halfway."

"Oh." I turn over a blobby gingerbread man. "I'd love to read it."

"Ack." Nelson swallows a lump of cookie. "Risk that you'll despise it: seriously high."

"Seriously low, I promise. But if you don't want me to, I understand."

"No, I *want* you to. I'm just worried you'll think I'm a total freakazoid."

Freaks. Über-cools. I glance over at Declan and Bridget. They're sitting together, sharing a piece of Meghann Foye's chocolate cheesecake. I can't tell—is Bridget now über-cool? Or is Declan a freak again? Or are they something in the middle?

Nelson pulls his notebook out of his bag. Before giving it to me, he says, "You'd . . . have to be honest, though. With what you thought. Don't say, 'Oh, I really liked it' if you think it rots."

And that makes me hesitate. Because what if I do hate it? And I say so? Won't Nelson hate my guts?

I ask him, "Doesn't that scare you? I don't think I could show someone something I did if I thought they might hate it."

"Yeah, but telling someone you love it doesn't mean you hate it any less."

"True. But you feel less crummy."

"No, you're just confused. Like, do they really like it? Are they lying? Is it any good, or am I fooling myself? I'd rather know the truth. Besides, if someone hates it, so what? Not gonna stop me from doing it."

That makes me think of all the kids who would immediately stop doing something if someone told them it was uncool—probably including me. I guess one of the advantages of being uncool is you never start worrying about that. Which is . . . cool.

I say, "I promise to be honest. But I'm also going to be nice."

"Sure." Nelson nods down at the book. "I mean, you are . . ."

All of a sudden, Eve plops down on the floor. "Aha, so this is where the real party is." She gives me a shove. "Many thanks for saving me from Manic Music Man."

I say in a lofty voice, "You should feel flattered that he wants you in chorus. We're a very elite group, you know."

"Yeah." Eve rolls her eyes. "So. Declan and Bridget."

"It's great."

"You're cool, I'm cool." She looks at Nelson. For a moment I can tell she's thinking, *Okay, my friend is sitting with a psycho*. Then she sticks out her hand. "Way to go, clocking Chris Abernathy."

Nelson smiles his lopsided smile. "Didn't . . . tray did."

Then someone almost steps on Eve, so she pushes closer to me. Which shoves me closer to Nelson. Who inches farther behind the desk. It becomes a game, with the three of us like train cars moving and bumping along until we're all behind the checkout desk, the noise of the party washing over our heads.

"This is definitely the place to be," says Eve.

"Definitely," I say. And Nelson nods.

That night after dinner I close my door and sit on my bed. Mouli immediately hops up and curls in beside me. He's figured out just where he has to be so that I can pet him without reaching. It's weird to think that just a few months ago he was too angry and scared to come out of his carrier. I still don't understand him all the time, but I get him, and that's what matters.

Usually when the semester ends, I worry. Did I say good-bye to everyone I should have? Did I do okay in my classes? Did I do anything dorky at the holiday party? This year I can't think of a single thing that went wrong. Which is really funny, when you consider my boyfriend dumped me for another girl. But I can't feel sad about it somehow. Declan didn't choose Bridget because she was more popular or hotter than me; he just liked her. Always did.

And if I'm honest, I don't know how much I ever liked Declan. As a boyfriend. I liked having him as my boyfriend, but we never had that much fun together. Okay, so I lost all pretension of being an über-cool, but having people like Chris Abernathy say hi to me isn't really the be-all and end-all.

I take *The Greatest Graphic Novel Ever* out of my bag and lift the cover. I really hope the first page isn't about some guy getting stabbed through the eyeball or shot a million times. And I really, really hope the guy doesn't look exactly like Chris Abernathy.

On the first page no one gets stabbed. No one gets shot.

Not on any of the other pages, either, although a few people do die. But that's right, I guess. People do die.

I read for two hours. When Russell bangs on my door, wanting to know if I'll play Game Boy with him, I say, "Later." When my mom asks if I want cocoa, I say, "Not now, thanks."

Then when I'm a third of the way through, I mark my place, close the book, and go to my computer. I write,

> Dear Nelson,
>   I think maybe you're right. You are a bit of a freakazoid.
>   But I also think you're maybe a bit of a genius.

I pick up *The Greatest Graphic Novel Ever* to find this one part I really liked. Something falls out of the pages. It's soft, dark, a little bit bigger than a quarter.

It's a petal. A dark red petal.

I pick it up, hold it up to the rose that's sitting on my desk.

It's a match.

FOURTEEN

THE IMAGE OF THE BOX

She who would the future know . . .

> Anna's To-Do List for Winter Break
> 1. Buy presents for Mom, Dad, Russell, Eve, Syd, and Mouli.
> 2. Discuss payment for babysitting Russell.
> 3. Read *Sense and Sensibility*.
> 4. Water Mr. Kaiser's plants.
> 5. PUT THE CARDS AWAY SOMEWHERE YOU WILL NEVER FIND THEM!

I put down the pencil and think. There must be something more I have to do, something more I can put on the list.

I pick up the pencil and write,

6. Who knows?

The first Saturday of winter break, Syd, Eve, and I get on the C train, which will take us to a place called Windsor Terrace, a man named Terence Joyce, and a cat named Tatiana.

As we wait to make the switch from the 1 to the C, Syd says, "Guys, what if it's a Beesley situation and one of us should take Tat home?"

I shake my head. "I can't do it." My mom has only just stopped calling Mouli "It."

Syd bites her lip. "My parents won't let me get another cat so soon on top of Beesley. And Beese needs a lot of attention."

We look at Eve, who says, "Not a pet person, sorry."

The first thing you see when you get off the train in Windsor Terrace is this beautiful park. It reminds me of Central Park, with old stone walls and rolling, sloping hills. I can totally imagine riding bikes there. It's quieter here, and the buildings are lower. You can actually see the sky. As we wander past a place called Terrace Bagels—there's a sign in the window: BEST BAGELS IN NY!—I think maybe Tatiana is happy here. Maybe Mr. Joyce has a big old chair next to a window that looks out on the park, and she sleeps on that chair all day.

Mr. Joyce lives on the top floor of a brownstone. I ring, then hear a voice say, "Hello?"

I call, "It's Anna, Syd, and Eve."

Unlike Mrs. Friedman's building, there is no elevator here, so we have to walk up two flights. Mr. Joyce is waiting for us at the top of the stairs. He's very tall and very thin—and very old. His ears are enormous and wrinkled. His hands are long; they shake a little as he waves hello. I'm a little nervous he might suddenly fall apart.

As Mr. Joyce leads us into his apartment, I look for Tatiana. I spot a big chair near a window, but the springs are hanging from the bottom and the seat sags.

No sign of Tatiana.

In a thin, dry voice, Mr. Joyce says, "Would you girls like tea?"

We look at one another. *Tea?* Then Syd says, "Yeah, that'd be great."

Mr. Joyce shambles into the kitchen, so we follow. "Please," he says, "have a seat. Oh—there are only two."

"I can stand," says Eve.

Mr. Joyce smiles as if he thinks that's a joke. "Can't have a lady standing." He pulls out the nearest chair for her; after a moment Eve sits down. Then he goes and gets a piano stool for me.

While Mr. Joyce fills up the teakettle, I say, "How did you know Mrs. Rosemont?"

"We were dancing partners." He puts the kettle on the stove.

Syd goes pink behind her freckles. "Dancing partners?"

"Yes." Mr. Joyce turns, does a little dance move. "At the Starlight Ballroom. Mrs. Rosemont's husband never liked to dance, so she went with me instead."

When the kettle whistles, Mr. Joyce starts making the tea. He doesn't use tea bags, I notice. Instead, he spoons tea straight from a box into a little ball, dunks the ball into a teapot, then pours hot water over it. Then he puts a funny quilted thing over the pot.

Eve says, "What's with the hat?"

"That is a tea cozy," he says calmly. "This is the only way to make tea. Ah, Madame Tatiana."

We look to see her standing at the entrance to the kitchen. I'd forgotten how beautiful she was, with pure white fur that radiates out from her body and imperious green eyes. She has enormous presence. But she looks a little out of place on the linoleum floor; in Mrs. Rosemont's apartment she barely ever budged from the couch, which had a velvet pillow on it just for her.

"Did Tatiana come with a pillow?" I ask Mr. Joyce as he sets out four teacups.

"A pillow? No. Just a carrier, very undignified."

Tatiana picks her way across the kitchen floor—lightly, as if she can't bear to walk on such a surface—and takes a few laps from a blue bowl on the floor.

"She definitely has star quality," says Eve, watching Tat settle by her chair.

"Mystique," agrees Mr. Joyce. "Cats are essentially unknowable. However much we want from them, they give only what they wish to."

That makes me think of Mouli, all the times I asked him what he thought. What is it about cats that makes you think they know things? What is it about them that makes you wish they could tell you what they know?

"Did you know you were going to . . ." Syd is trying not to refer to Mrs. Rosemont's death in any way. "Be living with Tatiana?"

"No." Mr. Joyce takes a sip of tea. "That was a surprise. Particularly for Luciano."

Eve looks around the apartment. "Luciano?"

"My African gray."

"You have a parrot?" says Syd.

"Oh, yes," says Mr. Joyce. "And I can't say he's been very happy with the arrival of Her Majesty. I've had to confine him to my study. No more walks about the apartment."

Appalled, Syd asks, "How could Mrs. Rosemont leave you a cat when she knew you had a parrot?"

"Oh, but she didn't know I had a parrot," explains Mr. Joyce. "It never came up."

Syd glances at me, and I say, "It's not very fair to Luciano. I mean, he was here first."

"Maybe not, but I don't know what else to do. I feel I can't give Tatiana away to a stranger. Etta gave her to me because she knew and trusted me. I couldn't betray that."

"Well, maybe it wouldn't have to be a stranger," I say. "Mrs. Rosemont left me one of the other cats. And Syd has Beesley."

Curious, Mr. Joyce looks at Eve, who says, "I didn't really know Mrs. Rosemont, sorry."

"Oh?" He sips his tea. "I'm sorry for you. She was a wonderful person to know."

For a little while we all drink our tea. It's impossible not to notice that Tatiana has chosen to sit by Eve's chair; she must sense the only other drama queen in the room.

"You have the same color eyes," Mr. Joyce remarks to her. "You and Tatiana."

Tatiana lifts her paw, bats the air. On any other creature, that might look like begging. But with Tat, it's a command—*Go, slave, fetch me my wrap.*

Syd and I look pleadingly at Eve. Mr. Joyce is a nice man, but he is very old, and with a parrot and linoleum . . . this just isn't the right place for Tat. She belongs with us, with her friends, Mouli and Beesley.

But Eve scowls. "Guys, come on. I'm not a take-care-of-things person."

Mr. Joyce says, "That's too bad."

"Well," says Eve sulkily, "I'm about all I can handle in the caretaking department."

He sips his tea. "But if you never care for something else, how do you know what caring is?"

"I have a pretty good idea," says Eve.

"Do you? Now, I've become accustomed to Luciano's needs, but they're very different from Tatiana's. She needs gracious surroundings—but nothing silly. Good food, but no big song and dance while it's served. She hates fuss. And she enjoys companionship, but she demands her privacy. In short, she needs respect and then love. Or perhaps, to put it better, the respect that comes from true love."

Eve looks down at Tatiana. Tatiana looks up at her.

Syd tells Eve, "Look, if it doesn't work out, I'll take her."

There's a long pause. Then Eve says, "No, she would hate that, being passed around from person to person like she wasn't worth anything. Wouldn't you?" she asks Tat.

At this, Tatiana tilts her head. It's not a commitment, but it's a "thinking about it." Which is more than she gives most people.

Eve tilts her head back. While the two of them carry on a haughtiness contest, I ask Mr. Joyce, "Do you miss Mrs. Rosemont?"

He nods. "Of course."

"I miss her too." As soon as I say it, I wonder, *Why?* Why should I miss a little old lady who talked too much? Who gave me old butterscotch candy and got lost in her own stories? Why should I miss someone I knew only for a little while?

I think of that timeline in Mr. Fegelson's classroom, the one that shows how short a time we've been on this earth. I look at Tat, now winding around Eve's legs; this will be her third home, her third human. I think of Beesley, who's so frail. Mr. Joyce, how his hand shakes as he sets the cup back on its saucer.

I don't know why I miss Mrs. Rosemont. I can't think of a single thing she did or said where I thought, *Wow! What an amazing person*. But I miss her. She was Mrs. Rosemont. And that's something to miss.

Plus, she gave me the cards. And what a weird ride that's been.

One thing about the cards? They lay things out in past, present, future. But you never know how long the future's going to last. That Lovers card could mean the rest of my life, it could mean a few weeks. If I did a reading now, Declan might not be part of it at all. The Page of Wands could be missing entirely. I tell myself that a few times; somehow, sitting in Mr. Joyce's kitchen, it hurts less than I thought it would.

Eve is still watching Tatiana. She knows she should take her. But Eve never does what she should; that's her rule.

But you can't have rules like that. Life is just way too complicated. I remember how Eve once made fun of my lists, saying, "What if something comes up that's not on the list?" I answered, "Anything that's important is going to be on my list."

And I was wrong. This whole thing with Declan and the cards has shown me you can think you know exactly what's going to happen and what you should do. Then it all goes haywire, and you just have to deal.

Eve asks Mr. Joyce, "Can I pet her?"

"I don't know," he says. "Why don't you try?"

As she reaches down, Tat stays perfectly still. Eve glances back at us. "Guys, this is nuts, you know that."

"Hey," I say. "Some things were meant to be."

The day before Christmas Eve—what Eve calls "Eve Eve"—Syd, Eve, and I get together to exchange presents. This year we're doing it at my house. And we're reuniting the cats for the first time.

I worried that Mouli would go back to his nasty old ways once he saw Beesley *and* Tatiana. But maybe because he's at my house—his house—he just looks at them like, *Oh, you*. And stays curled up on my bed. Tatiana, of course, stalks around the place like she owns it. Beesley never strays too far from Syd.

It's funny, Tat is perfect for Eve. And only Syd would know how to care for something as fragile as Beese. But I don't know how Mouli and I fit together. He's so temperamental, he could be with Eve. So in need of love, he could have gone to Syd. For a moment I have that old, sad feeling: Everyone's interesting except me.

Then all of a sudden, I feel a heavy paw on my leg,

then a thump as Mouli sits down on my lap. He swings his butt against me like, *Give me some room here.* I say, "I'm putting you on a diet, Mouli."

Syd laughs. "You guys are funny together. Wasn't he, like, your least favorite cat?"

"Yeah . . ." I look down at Mouli. "I guess he grows on you." But as I look around at the other cats, I realize that even if I had a choice, Mouli is the one I would want. Which is funny; I never would have said that a few months ago. Weird how things change.

"Present time," says Eve.

The way we do presents is each of us gets one for the other two. From Syd, I get a book called *How to Live with a Neurotic Cat*, which I open for Mouli to read. From Eve, I get an astrology guide. She says, "I figure, we have to switch dark arts. The cards totally blew it."

I think: *Not exactly.* I haven't told Eve and Syd about the rose petal I found in Nelson's book. I don't know what I think about it yet. And I don't want to talk about it before I do.

Then I hear Syd say, "The cards weren't wrong; she did end up with Declan."

"For, like, a second," says Eve.

"They never said I was going to be with him forever," I remind her. "And a lot of things in that reading did come true."

Because that's true, they did. The cards promised there would be competition—there was. Unhappiness—there was. Romance with a dark, young scholar—there was, and who knows, there might still be.

Syd says, "I still say I don't ever want to know what's going to happen. Why worry about something you can't change?"

"Because you *can* change it," I say, remembering all the crazy things I did. "You can change what you do. But not other people. Like Declan liking Bridget—there was no way I could stop that. But I'd rather know. I'd rather not be surprised."

"Declan was the imposter," sniffs Eve.

No, I think to myself, *I was. Or Declan and I were. And I'm glad we're not anymore.*

Then Eve says, "So, where are they?"

Even though I know what she means, I say, "Where are what?"

"The cards," says Syd.

"I put them away."

"Why?" asks Eve.

I laugh. "Don't you think they caused enough trouble? Declan . . . us fighting. I don't think we should touch them until we know what we're doing. Everything that went wrong went wrong because we didn't read the cards right."

For a moment Eve and Syd are quiet. Then Eve says, "But how will we learn if we never use them?"

Syd concentrates on petting Beesley. Now that we all feel they have some power, the cards scare her more than ever.

I say, "Well, I'm not doing another reading, that's for sure."

"No," says Syd. "You went already."

"It's our turn," says Eve.

I look at both of them, say, "Okay . . ."

I go to my closet. I reassemble the old encyclopedia set my dad had and climb up on it. Stretching my arm as far as it will go, I reach back on the top shelf. When I put the cards away, I wanted them to be hard to get. Guess what? I succeeded. For a second I think I'm going to have to get the stepladder, then the tips of my fingers brush old leather. I stand on my toes, get my hand on the box, and grab on.

Carefully stepping off the stack of encyclopedias, I sit back down on the rug with Syd and Eve. Mouli blinks sleepily from my lap.

"All right," I say. "Who's next?"

What's in the cards for
Anna, Eve, and Sydney?

Take a sneak peek at

In the Cards
Fame

The sad thing is, people want to be famous because they think it gives them an identity. That's just the biggest mistake—letting other people define who you are. As a performer, if you don't know your own worth before you start, you're not going to last very long.

—*Interview with Peter McElroy, judge for* You Suck!

"Who's next?"

Anna sets the cards in the center between us. Then she looks at me and Syd.

Syd immediately says, "Not me, no way. After what happened to you? Forget it." She frowns at the cards. "It's like they punish you for messing with stuff that's none of your business."

I say, "What do you mean, none of your business? It's *your* future."

Syd holds up her hand. "I'm just saying, maybe there are things we're not meant to know."

Annoyed, I reach for the box. If Syd wants to live her whole life in a chicken coop, fine. I'm asking my question.

Only I can't quite do it. I hate to admit it, but Syd's doom and gloom has me freaked. What if she's right? Anna went through serious craziness with her reading, and she just asked about a guy, not her whole entire life.

I turn to Anna. "Knowing what you know now, would you choose not to know?"

As Anna thinks, she picks up her cat, Mouli.

"The thing is, the cards only show you one small part of the future. Not the whole picture." One small part. Not the whole picture. But I want the whole picture. I want *Eve, you are on the road to fame and amazingness*. Not, *You'll get to sing at your cousin's bar mitzvah, and your Aunt Sadie will say you were great*. I want big time, bright lights, major, mondo success. I want to be one of those people you see at awards shows, the ones who win so many Grammys and Moonmen and nobody's even jealous because it's obvious they were so much better.

What if the cards say, *The closest you'll ever get to an awards show is watching it on TV while you stuff your face*.

I reach for the cards. Can't pick them up.

Anna nudges me. "Come on. We know what you want to ask."

"You don't have the first clue," I say irritably. I hate when people think they know things about me.

"Right." Anna leans down and says to the box "'Dear cards, will I be outrageously famous?'"

Okay, so maybe Anna does have the first clue.

"And what if they say no?" argues Syd, keeping her voice low so as not to disturb Beesley, who's asleep in her lap. "She should just give up, say, 'Fine, I'll be a garbage collector?'"

Anna says, "The cards only show you one version of the future. It's not unchangeable. Maybe they can show you what obstacles are in your way or people who can help you."

And maybe, I think, *they'll show you a life of blah nothingness.*

I put my hand on the box. It feels lifeless. No crackle of destiny or hum of the future. It's like the cards are taking a nap and I'm not important enough for them to wake up.

I glance at Tatiana. She's watching me, tail twitching. Her eyes say, *Don't do it*.

That's when I know in my gut: If I ask now, the cards will not give me the answer I want. The energy in the room is wrong, the planets aren't aligned right—whatever. It's not the right time.

I fold my arms. "No."

Shocked, Anna says, "What? Come on, I did it."

"I'll do it," I say stubbornly. "Just not right now."

"Do *not* tell me you're scared."

Okay, I won't tell you. "I'm not scared; the vibe's not right." Anna looks skeptical. "Look, it's winter break. Holiday craziness. If I do it now, all the cards are going to see in my future is my parents driving me insane and me pigging out. I have to wait."

"Until when?"

"I don't know," I say. "But it has to be the right time."

"You shouldn't do it if you don't want to," says Syd.

"I do want to," I howl. "Just *not now.*"

There's no one on the streets as I walk home. I guess because it's Christmas Eve—or Eve Eve, as I like to call it.

I walk past stores with fake snow sprayed on their windows, cardboard Santa Clauses, plastic holly—everything about this stupid season is fake.

And speaking of fake, man—best friends. They can be great but they also can be the most irritating people on earth.

What if they say you won't be famous?

We know what you want to ask.

I did a reading—why won't you?

I put on my headphones and blast music into my head. It's the only way I can get the voices to shut up. As I do, I imagine they're my songs, that I'm getting psyched up to a huge performance in front of a billion screaming fans.

In the elevator, I work out some moves. I like them so much, I keep dancing as I open the front door. I set Tat's carrier on the floor and let her out. She widens her eyes at my moves, then pads off. She's not into cheap flattery, I'll give her that.

I keep dancing down the hall—until I run smack into my brother, Mark, coming out of the bathroom.

Hello, major embarrassment.

Some people might be cool about it, might even dance along with you, you know? Not Mark. He's only three years older than me, but he acts like he's fifty. You should see his room. Not one single thing out of place. Bed made, clothing put away, books alphabetized, for God's sake. He's one of those people who has major school smarts, but is borderline retarded when it comes to life. I call him M.A.N. "Hey, man." "How you doing, man?" What Mark doesn't know is M.A.N. is my private code for Major Anal Nerd.

Now he's staring at me like I'm an intruder and he's wondering if he should call the cops. Which gets me past the embarrassment and right into annoyance.

I say, "Hey, *man*. What are you doing out of your room? You could catch cooties or something." I hold out my arm. "Ooh, look there's one jumping off of me . . ."

He sighs. "No self-respecting cootie would be caught dead on you."

First Anna and Syd—now Mark. Obviously, the universe has declared this "Pee on Eve Day." Actually, in this house every day is Pee on Eve Day. One of the reasons I cannot wait to get out of here.

Maybe I should have done the reading.

If you wanted proof that I share no DNA with the rest of my family, all you need to do is look at our rooms. Mark's and my parents' are tidy. Mine looks like a hurricane hit. But I like chaos. It suits my nature.

Kicking the mess out of the way, I ask Tat the question that's been pounding in my head all the way home. "Doing a reading would have been dumb, right? You knew it wasn't right." Tat widens her green eyes, as if to say, "Of course."

I sit down next to Tatiana, start petting her. You have to do it slowly, with respect. If Tat were human, she would definitely be famous. For one thing, she's gorgeous, with long silky white hair and the most beautiful eyes you ever saw. If I were half as beautiful as she is, I'd have it made. I feel like I got her in order to be reminded what real star power is.

Being a star means not letting anyone tell you what to do.

Being a star means you do it when you're ready and not a second before.

I will do a reading.